AN
OLD MAID

HONORE DE BALZAC

Translated By Katharine Prescott Wormeley

1st WORLD
LIBRARY
Literary Society

An Old Maid

Honore de Balzac

© 1st World Library – Literary Society, 2005
PO Box 2211
Fairfield, IA 52556
www.1stworldlibrary.org
First Edition

LCCN: 2005906492

Softcover ISBN: 1-4218-1548-6
Hardcover ISBN: 1-4218-1448-X
eBook ISBN: 1-4218-1648-2

Purchase *"An Old Maid"*
as a traditional bound book at:
www.1stWorldLibrary.org/purchase.asp?ISBN=1-4218-1548-6

1st World Library Literary Society is a nonprofit
organization dedicated to promoting literacy by:

- Creating a free internet library accessible from any
computer worldwide.
- Hosting writing competitions and offering book
publishing scholarships.

An Old Maid
contributed by Tim, Ed & Rodney
in support of
1st World Library Literary Society

DEDICATION

To Monsieur Eugene-Auguste-Georges-Louis
Midy de la Greneraye Surville,
Royal Engineer of the Ponts at Chausses.

As a testimony to the affection of his
brother-in-law, De Balzac

CHAPTER I

ONE OF MANY CHEVALIERS DE VALOIS

Most persons have encountered, in certain provinces in France, a number of Chevaliers de Valois. One lived in Normandy, another at Bourges, a third (with whom we have here to do) flourished in Alencon, and doubtless the South possesses others. The number of the Valesian tribe is, however, of no consequence to the present tale. All these chevaliers, among whom were doubtless some who were Valois as Louis XIV. was Bourbon, knew so little of one another that it was not advisable to speak to one about the others. They were all willing to leave the Bourbons in tranquil possession of the throne of France; for it was too plainly established that Henri IV. became king for want of a male heir in the first Orleans branch called the Valois. If there are any Valois, they descend from Charles de Valois, Duc d'Angouleme, son of Charles IX. and Marie Touchet, the male line from whom ended, until proof to the contrary be produced, in the person of the Abbe de Rothelin. The Valois-Saint-Remy, who descended from Henri II., also came to an end in the famous Lamothe-Valois implicated in the affair of the Diamond Necklace.

Each of these many chevaliers, if we may believe reports, was, like the Chevalier of Alencon, an old gentleman, tall, thin, withered, and moneyless. He of Bourges had emigrated; he of Touraine hid himself; he of Alencon fought in La Vendee and "chouanized" somewhat. The youth of the latter was spend in Paris, where the Revolution overtook him when thirty years of age in the midst of his conquests and gallantries.

The Chevalier de Valois of Alencon was accepted by the highest aristocracy of the province as a genuine Valois; and he distinguished himself, like the rest of his homonyms, by excellent manners, which proved him a man of society. He dined out every day, and played cards every evening. He was thought witty, thanks to his foible for relating a quantity of anecdotes on the reign of Louis XV. and the beginnings of the Revolution. When these tales were heard for the first time, they were held to be well narrated. He had, moreover, the great merit of not repeating his personal bons mots and of never speaking of his love-affairs, though his smiles and his airs and graces were delightfully indiscreet. The worthy gentleman used his privilege as a Voltairean noble to stay away from mass; and great indulgence was shown to his irreligion because of his devotion to the royal cause. One of his particular graces was the air and manner (imitated, no doubt, from Mole) with which he took snuff from a gold box adorned with the portrait of the Princess Goritza, - a charming Hungarian, celebrated for her beauty in the last years of the reign of Louis XV. Having been attached during his youth to that illustrious stranger, he still mentioned her with emotion. For her sake he had fought a duel with Monsieur de Lauzun.

The chevalier, now fifty-eight years of age, owned to only fifty; and he might well allow himself that innocent deception, for, among the other advantages granted to fair thin persons, he managed to preserve the still youthful figure which saves men as well as women from an appearance of old age. Yes, remember this: all of life, or rather all the elegance that expresses life, is in the figure. Among the chevalier's other possessions must be counted an enormous nose with which nature had endowed him. This nose vigorously divided a pale face into two sections which seemed to have no knowledge of each other, for one side would redden under the process of digestion, while the other continued white. This fact is worthy of remark at a period when physiology is so busy with the human heart. The incandescence, so to call it, was on the left side. Though his long slim legs, supporting a lank body, and his pallid skin, were not indicative of health, Monsieur de Valois ate like an ogre and declared he had a malady called in the provinces "hot liver," perhaps to excuse his monstrous appetite. The circumstance of his singular flush confirmed this declaration; but in a region where repasts are developed on the line of thirty or forty dishes and last four hours, the chevalier's stomach would seem to have been a blessing bestowed by Providence on the good town of Alencon. According to certain doctors, heat on the left side denotes a prodigal heart. The chevalier's gallantries confirmed this scientific assertion, the responsibility for which does not rest, fortunately, on the historian.

In spite of these symptoms, Monsieur de Valois' constitution was vigorous, consequently long-lived. If his liver "heated," to use an old-fashioned word, his heart was not less inflammable. His face was wrinkled and his hair silvered; but an intelligent observer would have recognized at once the stigmata of passion and the furrows of pleasure which appeared in the crow's-feet and the marches-du-palais, so prized at the court of Cythera. Everything about this dainty chevalier bespoke the "ladies' man." He was so minute in his ablutions that his cheeks were a pleasure to look upon; they seemed to have been laved in some miraculous water. The part of his skull which his hair refused to cover shone like ivory. His eyebrows, like his hair, affected youth by the care and regularity with which they were combed. His skin, already white, seemed to have been extra-whitened by some secret compound. Without using perfumes, the chevalier exhaled a certain fragrance of youth, that refreshed the atmosphere. His hands, which were those of a gentleman, and were cared for like the hands of a pretty woman, attracted the eye to their rosy, well-shaped nails. In short, had it not been for his magisterial and stupendous nose, the chevalier might have been thought a trifle too dainty.

We must here compel ourselves to spoil this portrait by the avowal of a littleness. The chevalier put cotton in his ears, and wore, appended to them, two little earrings representing negroes' heads in diamonds, of admirable workmanship. He clung to these singular appendages, explaining that since his ears had been bored he had ceased to have headaches (he had had headaches). We do not present the chevalier as an accomplished man; but surely we can pardon, in an old celibate whose heart sends so much blood to his left cheek, these adorable qualities, founded, perhaps, on some sublime secret history.

Besides, the Chevalier de Valois redeemed those negroes' heads by so many other graces that society felt itself sufficiently compensated. He really took such immense trouble to conceal his age and give pleasure to his friends. In the first place, we must call attention to the extreme care he gave to his linen, the only distinction that well-bred men can nowadays exhibit in their clothes. The linen of the chevalier was invariably of a fineness and whiteness that were truly aristocratic. As for his coat, though remarkable for its cleanliness, it was always half worn-out, but without spots or creases. The preservation of that garment was something marvellous to those who noticed the chevalier's high-bred indifference to its shabbiness. He did not go so far as to scrape the seams with glass, - a refinement invented by the Prince of Wales; but he did practice the rudiments of English elegance with a personal satisfaction little understood by the people of Alencon. The world owes a great deal to persons who take such pains to please it. In this there is certainly some accomplishment of that most difficult precept of the Gospel about rendering good for evil. This freshness of ablution and all the other little cares harmonized charmingly with the blue eyes, the ivory teeth, and the blond person of the old chevalier.

The only blemish was that this retired Adonis had nothing manly about him; he seemed to be employing this toilet varnish to hide the ruins occasioned by the military service of gallantry only. But we must hasten to add that his voice produced what might be called an antithesis to his blond delicacy. Unless you adopted the opinion of certain observers of the human heart, and thought that the chevalier had the voice of his nose, his organ of speech would have amazed you by its full and redundant sound. Without possessing the volume of classical bass voices, the tone of it was pleasing from a slightly muffled quality like that of an English bugle, which is firm and sweet, strong but velvety.

The chevalier had repudiated the ridiculous costume still preserved by certain monarchical old men; he had frankly modernized himself. He was always seen in a maroon-colored coat with gilt buttons, half-tight breeches of poult-de-soie with gold buckles, a white waistcoat without embroidery, and a tight cravat showing no shirt-collar, - a last vestige of the old French costume which he did not renounce, perhaps, because it enabled him to show a neck like that of the sleekest abbe. His shoes were noticeable for their square buckles, a style of which the present generation has no knowledge; these buckles were fastened to a square of polished black leather. The chevalier allowed two watch-chains to hang parallel to each other from each of his waistcoat pockets, - another vestige of the eighteenth century, which the Incroyables had not disdained to use under the Directory. This transition costume, uniting as it did two centuries, was worn by the chevalier with the high-bred grace of an old French marquis, the secret of which is lost to France since the day when Fleury, Mole's last pupil, vanished.

The private life of this old bachelor was apparently open to all eyes, though in fact it was quite mysterious. He lived in a lodging that was modest, to say the best of it, in the rue du Cours, on the second floor of a house belonging to Madame Lardot, the best and busiest washerwoman in the town. This circumstance will explain the excessive nicety of his linen. Ill-luck would have it that the day came when Alencon was guilty of believing that the chevalier had not always comported himself as a gentleman should, and that in fact he was secretly married in his old age to a certain Cesarine, - the mother of a child which had had the impertinence to come into the world without being called for.

"He had given his hand," as a certain Monsieur du Bousquier remarked, "to the person who had long had him under irons."

This horrible calumny embittered the last days of the dainty chevalier all the more because, as the present Scene will show, he had lost a hope long cherished to which he had made many sacrifices.

Madame Lardot leased to the chevalier two rooms on the second floor of her house, for the modest sum of one hundred francs a year. The worthy gentleman dined out every day, returning only in time to go to bed. His sole expense therefore was for breakfast, invariably composed of a cup of chocolate, with bread and butter and fruits in their season. He made no fire except in the coldest winter, and then only enough to get up by. Between eleven and four o'clock he walked about, went to read the papers, and paid visits. From the time of his settling in Alencon he had nobly admitted his poverty, saying that his whole fortune consisted in an annuity of six hundred francs a year, the sole remains of his former opulence, - a property which obliged him to see his man of business (who held the annuity papers) quarterly. In truth, one of the Alencon bankers paid him every three months one hundred and fifty francs, sent down by Monsieur Bordin of Paris, the last of the *procureurs du Chatelet*. Every one knew these details because the chevalier exacted the utmost secrecy from the persons to whom he first confided them.

Monsieur de Valois gathered the fruit of his misfortunes. His place at table was laid in all the most distinguished houses in Alencon, and he was bidden to all soirees. His talents as a card-player, a narrator, an amiable man of the highest breeding, were so well known and appreciated that parties would have seemed a failure if the dainty connoisseur was absent. Masters of houses and their wives felt the need of his approving grimace. When a young woman heard the chevalier say at a ball, "You are delightfully well-dressed!" she was more pleased at such praise than she would have been at mortifying a rival. Monsieur de Valois was the only man who could perfectly pronounce certain phrases of the olden time. The words, "my heart," "my jewel," "my little pet," "my queen," and the amorous diminutives of 1770, had a grace that was quite irresistible when they came from his lips. In short, the chevalier had the privilege of superlatives. His compliments, of which he was stingy, won the good graces of all the old women; he made himself agreeable to every one, even to the officials of the government, from whom he wanted nothing. His behavior at cards had a lofty distinction which everybody noticed: he never complained; he praised his adversaries when they lost; he did not rebuke or teach his partners by showing them how they ought to have played. When, in the course of a deal, those sickening dissertations on the game would take place, the chevalier invariably drew out his snuff-box with a gesture that was worthy of Mole, looked at the Princess Goritza, raised the cover with dignity, shook, sifted, massed the snuff, and gathered his pinch, so that by the time the cards were dealt he had decorated both nostrils and replaced the princess in his waistcoat pocket, - always on his left side. A gentleman of the "good" century (in distinction from the "grand" century) could alone have invented that compromise between contemptuous silence and a sarcasm which might not have been understood. He accepted poor players and knew how to make the best of them. His delightful equability of temper made

Honore de Balzac

many persons say, -

"I do admire the Chevalier de Valois!"

His conversation, his manners, seemed bland, like his person. He endeavored to shock neither man nor woman. Indulgent to defects both physical and mental, he listened patiently (by the help of the Princess Goritza) to the many dull people who related to him the petty miseries of provincial life, - an egg ill-boiled for breakfast, coffee with feathered cream, burlesque details about health, disturbed sleep, dreams, visits. The chevalier could call up a languishing look, he could take on a classic attitude to feign compassion, which made him a most valuable listener; he could put in an "Ah!" and a "Bah!" and a "What DID you do?" with charming appropriateness. He died without any one suspecting him of even an allusion to the tender passages of his romance with the Princess Goritza. Has any one ever reflected on the service a dead sentiment can do to society; how love may become both social and useful? This will serve to explain why, in spite of his constant winning at play (he never left a salon without carrying off with him about six francs), the old chevalier remained the spoilt darling of the town. His losses - which, by the bye, he always proclaimed, were very rare.

All who know him declare that they have never met, not even in the Egyptian museum at Turin, so agreeable a mummy. In no country in the world did parasitism ever take on so pleasant a form. Never did selfishness of a most concentrated kind appear less forth-putting, less offensive, than in this old gentleman; it stood him in place of devoted friendship. If some one asked Monsieur de Valois to do him a little service which might have discommoded him, that some one did not part from the worthy chevalier without being truly enchanted with him, and quite convinced that he either could not do the service demanded, or that he should injure the affair if he meddled in it.

To explain the problematic existence of the chevalier, the historian, whom Truth, that cruel wanton, grasps by the throat, is compelled to say that after the "glorious" sad days of July, Alencon discovered that the chevalier's nightly winnings amounted to about one hundred and fifty francs every three months; and that the clever old nobleman had had the pluck to send to himself his annuity in order not to appear in the eyes of a community, which loves the main chance, to be entirely without resources. Many of his friends (he was by that time dead, you will please remark) have contested mordicus this curious fact, declaring it to be a fable, and upholding the Chevalier de Valois as a respectable and worthy gentleman whom the liberals calumniated. Luckily for shrewd players, there are people to be found among the spectators who will always sustain them. Ashamed of having to defend a piece of wrong-doing, they stoutly deny it. Do not accuse them of wilful infatuation; such men have a sense of their dignity; governments set them the example of a virtue which consists in burying their dead without chanting the Misere of their defeats. If the chevalier did allow himself this bit of shrewd practice, - which, by the bye, would have won him the regard of the Chevalier de Gramont, a smile from the Baron de Foeneste, a shake of the hand from the Marquis de Moncade, - was he any the less that amiable guest, that witty talker, that imperturbable card-player, that famous teller of anecdotes, in whom all Alencon took delight? Besides, in what way was this action, which is certainly within the rights of a man's own will, - in what way was it contrary to the ethics of a gentleman? When so many persons are forced to pay annuities to others, what more natural than to pay one to his own best friend? But Laius is dead -

To return to the period of which we are writing: after about fifteen years of this way of life the chevalier had amassed ten thousand and some odd hundred francs. On the return of the Bourbons, one of his old friends, the Marquis de Pombreton, formerly lieutenant in the Black mousquetaires, returned to him - so he said - twelve hundred pistoles which he had lent to the marquis for the purpose of emigrating. This event made a sensation; it was used later to refute the sarcasms of the "Constitutionnel," on the method employed by some emigres in paying their debts. When this noble act of the Marquis de Pombreton was lauded before the chevalier, the good man reddened even to his right cheek. Every one rejoiced frankly at this windfall for Monsieur de Valois, who went about consulting moneyed people as to the safest manner of investing this fragment of his past opulence. Confiding in the future of the Restoration, he finally placed his money on the Grand-Livre at the moment when the funds were at fifty-six francs and twenty-five centimes. Messieurs de Lenoncourt, de Navarreins, de Verneuil, de Fontaine, and La Billardiere, to whom he was known, he said, obtained for him, from the king's privy purse, a pension of three hundred francs, and sent him, moreover, the cross of Saint-Louis. Never was it known positively by what means the old chevalier obtained these two solemn consecrations of his title and merits. But one thing is certain; the cross of

Saint-Louis authorized him to take the rank of retired colonel in view of his service in the Catholic armies of the West.

Besides his fiction of an annuity, about which no one at the present time knew anything, the chevalier really had, therefore, a bona fide income of a thousand francs. But in spite of this bettering of his circumstances, he made no change in his life, manners, or appearance, except that the red ribbon made a fine effect on his maroon-colored coat, and completed, so to speak, the physiognomy of a gentleman. After 1802, the chevalier sealed his letters with a very old seal, ill-engraved to be sure, by which the Casterans, the d'Esgrignons, the Troisvilles were enabled to see that he bore: *Party of France, two cottises gemelled gules, and gules, five mascles or, placed end to end; on a chief sable, a cross argent*. For crest, a knight's helmet. For motto: "Valeo." Bearing such noble arms, the so-called bastard of the Valois had the right to get into all the royal carriages of the world.

Many persons envied the quiet existence of this old bachelor, spent on whist, boston, backgammon, reversi, and piquet, all well played, on dinners well digested, snuff gracefully inhaled, and tranquil walks about the town. Nearly all Alencon believed this life to be exempt from ambitions and serious interests; but no man has a life as simple as envious neighbors attribute to him. You will find in the most out-of-the way villages human mollusks, creatures apparently dead, who have passions for lepidoptera or for conchology, let us say, - beings who will give themselves infinite pains about moths, butter-flies, or the concha Veneris. Not only did the chevalier have his own particular shells, but he cherished an ambitious desire which he

Honore de Balzac

pursued with a craft so profound as to be worthy of Sixtus the Fifth: he wanted to marry a certain rich old maid, with the intention, no doubt, of making her a stepping-stone by which to reach the more elevated regions of the court. There, then, lay the secret of his royal bearing and of his residence in Alencon.

CHAPTER II

SUSANNAH AND THE ELDERS

On a Wednesday morning, early, toward the middle of spring, in the year 16, - such was his mode of reckoning, - at the moment when the chevalier was putting on his old green-flowered damask dressing-gown, he heard, despite the cotton in his ears, the light step of a young girl who was running up the stairway. Presently three taps were discreetly struck upon the door; then, without waiting for any response, a handsome girl slipped like an eel into the room occupied by the old bachelor.

"Ah! is it you, Suzanne?" said the Chevalier de Valois, without discontinuing his occupation, which was that of stropping his razor. "What have you come for, my dear little jewel of mischief?"

"I have come to tell you something which may perhaps give you as much pleasure as pain?"

"Is it anything about Cesarine?"

"Cesarine! much I care about your Cesarine!" she said with a saucy air, half serious, half indifferent.

This charming Suzanne, whose present comical

Honore de Balzac

performance was to exercise a great influence in the principal personages of our history, was a work-girl at Madame Lardot's. One word here on the topography of the house. The wash-rooms occupied the whole of the ground floor. The little courtyard was used to hang out on wire cords embroidered handkerchiefs, collarets, capes, cuffs, frilled shirts, cravats, laces, embroidered dresses, - in short, all the fine linen of the best families of the town. The chevalier assumed to know from the number of her capes in the wash how the love-affairs of the wife of the prefect were going on. Though he guessed much from observations of this kind, the chevalier was discretion itself; he was never betrayed into an epigram (he had plenty of wit) which might have closed to him an agreeable salon. You are therefore to consider Monsieur de Valois as a man of superior manners, whose talents, like those of many others, were lost in a narrow sphere. Only - for, after all, he was a man - he permitted himself certain penetrating glances which could make some women tremble; although they all loved him heartily as soon as they discovered the depth of his discretion and the sympathy that he felt for their little weaknesses.

The head woman, Madame Lardot's factotum, an old maid of forty-six, hideous to behold, lived on the opposite side of the passage to the chevalier. Above them were the attics where the linen was dried in winter. Each apartment had two rooms, - one lighted from the street, the other from the courtyard. Beneath the chevalier's room there lived a paralytic, Madame Lardot's grandfather, an old buccaneer named Grevin, who had served under Admiral Simeuse in India, and was now stone-deaf. As for Madame Lardot, who occupied the other lodging on the first floor, she had so great a weakness for persons of condition that she may well have been thought blind to the ways of the chevalier. To her, Monsieur de Valois was a despotic monarch who did right in all things. Had any of her workwomen been guilty of a happiness attributed to the chevalier she would have said, "He is so lovable!" Thus, though the house was of glass, like all provincial houses, it was discreet as a robber's cave.

A born confidant to all the little intrigues of the work-rooms, the chevalier never passed the door, which usually stood open, without giving something to his little ducks, - chocolate, bonbons, ribbons, laces, gilt crosses, and such like trifles adored by grisettes; consequently, the kind old gentleman was adored in return. Women have an instinct which enables them to divine the men who love them, who like to be near them, and exact no payment for gallantries. In this respect women have the instinct of dogs, who in a mixed company will go straight to the man to whom animals are sacred.

The poor Chevalier de Valois retained from his former life the need of bestowing gallant protection, a quality of the seigneurs of other days. Faithful to the system of the "petite maison," he liked to enrich women, - the only beings who know how to receive, because they can always return. But the poor chevalier could no longer ruin himself for a mistress. Instead of the choicest bonbons wrapped in bank-bills, he gallantly presented paper-bags full of toffee. Let us say to the glory of Alencon that the toffee was accepted with more joy than la Duthe ever showed at a gilt service or a fine equipage offered by the Comte d'Artois. All these grisettes fully understood the fallen majesty of the Chevalier de Valois, and they kept their private familiarities with him a profound secret for his sake. If they were questioned about him in certain houses when they carried home the linen, they always spoke respectfully of the chevalier, and made him out older than he really was; they talked of him as a most respectable monsieur, whose life was a flower of sanctity; but once in their own regions they perched on his shoulders like so many parrots. He liked to be told the secrets which washerwomen discover in the bosom of households, and day after day these girls would tell him the cancans which were going the round of Alencon. He called them his "petticoat gazettes," his "talking feuilletons." Never did Monsieur de Sartines have spies more intelligent and less expensive, or minions who showed more honor while displaying their rascality of mind. So it may be said that in the mornings, while breakfasting, the chevalier usually amused himself as much as the saints in heaven.

Suzanne was one of his favorites, a clever, ambitious girl, made of the stuff of a Sophie Arnold, and handsome withal, as the handsomest courtesan invited by Titian to pose on black velvet for a model of Venus; although her face, fine about the eyes and forehead, degenerated, lower down, into commonness of outline. Hers was a Norman beauty, fresh, high-colored, redundant, the flesh of Rubens covering the muscles of the Farnese Hercules, and not the slender articulations of the Venus de' Medici, Apollo's graceful consort.

"Well, my child, tell me your great or your little adventure, whatever it is."

The particular point about the chevalier which would have made him noticeable from Paris to Pekin, was the gentle paternity of his manner to grisettes. They reminded him of the illustrious operatic queens of his early days, whose celebrity was European during a good third of the eighteenth century. It is certain that the old gentleman, who had lived in days gone by with that feminine nation now as much forgotten as many other great things, - like the Jesuits, the Buccaneers, the Abbes, and the Farmers-General, - had acquired an irresistible good-humor, a kindly ease, a laisser-aller devoid of egotism, the self-effacement of Jupiter with Alcmene, of the king intending to be duped, who casts his thunderbolts to the devil, wants his Olympus full of follies, little suppers, feminine profusions - but with Juno out of the way, be it understood.

In spite of his old green damask dressing-gown and the bareness of the room in which he sat, where the floor was covered with a shabby tapestry in place of carpet, and the walls were hung with tavern-paper presenting the profiles of Louis XVI. and members of his family, traced among the branches of a weeping willow with other sentimentalities invented by royalism during the Terror, - in spite of his ruins, the chevalier, trimming his beard before a shabby old toilet-table, draped with trumpery lace, exhaled an essence of the eighteenth century. All the libertine graces of his youth reappeared; he seemed to have the wealth of three hundred thousand francs of debt, while his vis-a-vis waited before the door. He was grand, - like Berthier on the retreat from Moscow, issuing orders to an army that existed no longer.

"Monsieur le chevalier," replied Suzanne, drolly, "seems to me I needn't tell you anything; you've only to look."

And Suzanne presented a side view of herself which gave a sort of lawyer's comment to her words. The chevalier, who, you must know, was a sly old bird, lowered his right eye on the grisette, still holding the razor at his throat, and pretended to understand.

"Well, well, my little duck, we'll talk about that presently. But you are rather previous, it seems to me."

"Why, Monsieur le chevalier, ought I to wait until my mother beats me and Madame Lardot turns me off? If I don't get away soon to Paris, I shall never be able to marry here, where men are so ridiculous."

"It can't be helped, my dear; society is changing; women are just as much victims to the present state of things as the nobility themselves. After political overturn comes the overturn of morals. Alas! before long woman won't exist" (he took out the cotton-wool to arrange his ears): "she'll lose everything by rushing into sentiment; she'll wring her nerves; good-bye to all the good little pleasures of our time, desired without shame, accepted without nonsense." (He polished up the little negroes' heads.) "Women had hysterics in those days to get their ends, but now" (he began to laugh) "their vapors end in charcoal. In short, marriage" (here he picked up his pincers to remove a hair) "will become a thing intolerable; whereas it used to be so gay in my day! The reigns of Louis XIV. and Louis XV. - remember this, my child - said farewell to the finest manners and morals ever known to the world."

"But, Monsieur le chevalier," said the grisette, "the matter now concerns the morals and honor of your poor little Suzanne, and I hope you won't abandon her."

"Abandon her!" cried the chevalier, finishing his hair; "I'd sooner abandon my own name."

"Ah!" exclaimed Suzanne.

"Now, listen to me, you little mischief," said the chevalier, sitting down on a huge sofa, formerly called a duchesse, which Madame Lardot had been at some pains to find for him.

He drew the magnificent Suzanne before him, holding her legs between his knees. She let him do as he liked, although in the street she was offish enough to other men, refusing their familiarities partly from decorum and partly for contempt for their commonness. She now stood audaciously in front of the chevalier, who, having fathomed in his day many other mysteries in minds that were far more wily, took in the situation at a single glance. He knew very well that no young girl would joke about a real dishonor; but he took good care not to knock over the pretty scaffolding of her lie as he touched it.

"We slander ourselves," he said with inimitable craft; "we are as virtuous as that beautiful biblical girl whose name we bear; we can always marry as we please, but we are thirsty for Paris, where charming creatures - and we are no fool - get rich without trouble. We want to go and see if the great capital of pleasures hasn't some young Chevalier de Valois in store for us, with a carriage, diamonds, an opera-box, and so forth. Russians, Austrians, Britons, have millions on which we have an eye. Besides, we are patriotic; we want to help France in getting back her money from the pockets of those gentry. Hey! hey! my dear little devil's duck! it isn't a bad plan. The world you live in may cry out a bit, but success justifies all things. The worst thing in this world, my dear, is to be without money; that's our disease, yours and mine. Now inasmuch as we have plenty of wit, we thought it would be a good thing to parade our dear little honor, or dishonor, to catch an old boy; but that old boy, my dear heart, knows the Alpha and Omega of female tricks, - which means that you could easier put salt on a sparrow's tail than to make me believe I have anything to do with your little affair. Go to Paris, my dear; go at the cost of an old celibate, I won't prevent it; in fact, I'll help you, for an old bachelor, Suzanne, is the natural money-box of a young girl. But don't drag me into the matter. Listen, my queen, you who know life pretty well; you would me great harm and give me much pain, - harm, because you would prevent my marriage in a town where people cling to morality; pain, because if you are in trouble (which I deny, you sly puss!) I haven't a penny to get you out of it. I'm as poor as a church mouse; you know that, my dear. Ah! if I marry Mademoiselle Cormon, if I am once more rich, of course I would prefer you to Cesarine. You've always seemed to me as fine as the gold they gild on lead; you were made to be the love of a great seigneur. I think you so clever that the trick you are trying to play off on me doesn't surprise me one bit; I expected it. You are flinging the scabbard after the sword, and that's daring for a girl. It takes nerve and superior ideas to do it, my angel, and therefore you have won my respectful esteem."

"Monsieur le chevalier, I assure you, you are mistaken, and -"

She colored, and did not dare to say more. The chevalier, with a single glance, had guessed and fathomed her whole plan.

"Yes, yes! I understand: you want me to believe it," he said. "Well! I do believe it. But take my advice: go to Monsieur du Bousquier. Haven't you taken linen there for the last six or eight months? I'm not asking what went on between you; but I know the man: he has immense conceit; he is an old bachelor, and very rich; and he only spends a quarter of a comfortable income. If you are as clever as I suppose, you can go to Paris at his expense. There, run along, my little doe; go and twist him round your finger. Only, mind this: be as supple as silk; at every word take a double turn round him and make a knot. He is a man to fear scandal, and if he has given you a chance to put him in the pillory - in short, understand; threaten him with the ladies of the Maternity Hospital. Besides, he's ambitious. A man succeeds through his wife, and you are handsome and clever enough to make the fortune of a husband. Hey! the mischief! you could hold your own against all the court ladies."

Suzanne, whose mind took in at a flash the chevalier's last words, was eager to run off to du Bousquier, but, not wishing to depart too abruptly, she questioned the chevalier about Paris, all the while helping him to dress. The chevalier, however, divined her desire to be off, and favored it by asking her to tell Cesarine to bring up his chocolate, which Madame Lardot made for him every morning. Suzanne then slipped away to her new victim, whose biography must here be given.

Born of an old Alencon family, du Bousquier was a cross between the bourgeois and the country squire. Finding himself without means on the death of his father, he went, like other ruined provincials, to Paris.

On the breaking out of the Revolution he took part in public affairs. In spite of revolutionary principles, which made a hobby of republican honesty, the management of public business in those days was by no means clean. A political spy, a stock-jobber, a contractor, a man who confiscated in collusion with the syndic of a commune the property of emigres in order to sell them and buy them in, a minister, and a general were all equally engaged in public business. From 1793 to 1799 du Bousquier was commissary of provisions to the French armies. He lived in a magnificent hotel and was one of the matadors of finance, did business with Ouvrard, kept open house, and led the scandalous life of the period, - the life of a Cincinnatus, on sacks of corn harvested without trouble, stolen rations, "little houses" full of mistresses, in which were given splendid fetes to the Directors of the Republic.

The citizen du Bousquier was one of Barras' familiars; he was on the best of terms with Fouche, stood very well with Bernadotte, and fully expected to become a minister by throwing himself into the party which secretly caballed against Bonaparte until Marengo. If it had not been for Kellermann's charge and Desaix's death, du Bousquier would probably have become a minister. He was one of the chief assistances of that secret government whom Napoleon's luck send behind the scenes in 1793. (See "An Historical Mystery.") The unexpected victory of Marengo was the defeat of that party who actually had their proclamations printed to return to the principles of the Montagne in case the First Consul succumbed.

Convinced of the impossibility of Bonaparte's triumph, du Bousquier staked the greater part of his property on a fall in the Funds, and kept two couriers on the field of battle. The first started for Paris when Melas' victory was certain; the second, starting four hours later, brought the news of the defeat of the Austrians. Du Bousquier cursed Kellermann and Desaix; he dared not curse Bonaparte, who might owe him millions. This alternative of millions to be earned and present ruin staring him in the face, deprived the purveyor of most of his faculties: he became nearly imbecile for several days; the man had so abused his health by excesses that when the thunderbolt fell upon him he had no strength to resist. The payment of his bills against the Exchequer gave him some hopes for the future, but, in spite of all efforts to ingratiate himself, Napoleon's hatred to the contractors who had speculated on his defeat made itself felt; du Bousquier was left without a sou. The immorality of his private life, his intimacy with Barras and Bernadotte, displeased the First Consul even more than his manoeuvres at the Bourse, and he struck du Bousquier's name from the list of the government contractors.

Out of all his past opulence du Bousquier saved only twelve hundred francs a year from an investment in the Grand Livre, which he had happened to place there by pure caprice, and which saved him from penury. A man ruined by the First Consul interested the town of Alencon, to which he now returned, where royalism was secretly dominant. Du Bousquier, furious against Bonaparte, relating stories against him of his mean-ness, of Josephine's improprieties, and all the other scandalous anecdotes of the last ten years, was well received.

About this time, when he was somewhere between forty and fifty, du Bousquier's appearance was that of a

Honore de Balzac

bachelor of thirty-six, of medium height, plump as a purveyor, proud of his vigorous calves, with a strongly marked countenance, a flattened nose, the nostrils garnished with hair, black eyes with thick lashes, from which darted shrewd glances like those of Monsieur de Talleyrand, though somewhat dulled. He still wore republican whiskers and his hair very long; his hands, adorned with bunches of hair on each knuckle, showed the power of his muscular system in their prominent blue veins. He had the chest of the Farnese Hercules, and shoulders fit to carry the stocks. Such shoulders are seen nowadays only at Tortoni's. This wealth of masculine vigor counted for much in du Bousquier's relations with others. And yet in him, as in the chevalier, symptoms appeared which contrasted oddly with the general aspect of their persons. The late purveyor had not the voice of his muscles. We do not mean that his voice was a mere thread, such as we sometimes hear issuing from the mouth of these walruses; on the contrary, it was a strong voice, but stifled, an idea of which can be given only by comparing it with the noise of a saw cutting into soft and moistened wood, - the voice of a worn-out speculator.

In spite of the claims which the enmity of the First Consul gave Monsieur du Bousquier to enter the royalist society of the province, he was not received in the seven or eight families who composed the faubourg Saint-Germain of Alencon, among whom the Chevalier de Valois was welcome. He had offered himself in marriage, through her notary, to Mademoiselle Armande, sister of the most distinguished noble in the town; to which offer he received a refusal. He consoled himself as best he could in the society of a dozen rich families, former manufacturers of the old point d'Alencon, owners of pastures and cattle, or merchants doing a wholesale business in linen, among whom, as he hoped, he might find a wealthy wife. In fact, all his hopes now converged to the perspective of a fortunate marriage. He was not without a certain financial ability, which many persons used to their profit. Like a ruined gambler who advises neophytes, he pointed out enterprises and speculations, together with the means and chances of conducting them. He was thought a good administrator, and it was often a question of making him mayor of Alencon; but the memory of his underhand jobbery still clung to him, and he was never received at the prefecture. All the succeeding governments, even that of the Hundred Days, refused to appoint him mayor of Alencon, - a place he coveted, which, could he have had it, would, he thought, have won him the hand of a certain old maid on whom his matrimonial views now turned.

Du Bousquier's aversion to the Imperial government had thrown him at first into the royalist circles of Alencon, where he remained in spite of the rebuffs he received there; but when, after the first return of the Bourbons, he was still excluded from the prefecture, that mortification inspired him with a hatred as deep as it was secret against the royalists. He now returned to his old opinions, and became the leader of the liberal party in Alencon, the invisible manipulator of elections, and did immense harm to the Restoration by the cleverness of his underhand proceedings and the perfidy of his outward behavior. Du Bousquier, like all those who live by their heads only, carried on his hatreds with the quiet tranquillity of a rivulet, feeble apparently, but inexhaustible. His hatred was that of a negro, so peaceful that it deceived the enemy. His vengeance, brooded over for fifteen years, was as yet satisfied by no victory, not even that of

July, 1830.

It was not without some private intention that the Chevalier de Valois had turned Suzanne's designs upon Monsieur du Bousquier. The liberal and the royalist had mutually divined each other in spite of the wide dissimulation with which they hid their common hope from the rest of the town. The two old bachelors were secretly rivals. Each had formed a plan to marry the Demoiselle Cormon, whom Monsieur de Valois had mentioned to Suzanne. Both, ensconced in their idea and wearing the armor of apparent indifference, awaited the moment when some lucky chance might deliver the old maid over to them. Thus, if the two old bachelors had not been kept asunder by the two political systems of which they each offered a living expression, their private rivalry would still have made them enemies. Epochs put their mark on men. These two individuals proved the truth of that axiom by the opposing historic tints that were visible in their faces, in their conversation, in their ideas, and in their clothes. One, abrupt, energetic, with loud, brusque manners, curt, rude speech, dark in tone, in hair, in look, terrible apparently, in reality as impotent as an insurrection, represented the republic admirably. The other, gentle and polished, elegant and nice, attaining his ends by the slow and infallible means of diplomacy, faithful to good taste, was the express image of the old courtier regime.

The two enemies met nearly every evening on the same ground. The war was courteous and benign on the side of the chevalier; but du Bousquier showed less ceremony on his, though still preserving the outward appearances demanded by society, for he did not wish to be driven from the place. They themselves fully understood each other; but in spite of the shrewd observation which provincials bestow on the petty interests of their own little centre, no one in the town suspected the rivalry of these two men. Monsieur le Chevalier de Valois occupied a vantage-ground: he had never asked for the hand of Mademoiselle Cormon; whereas du Bousquier, who entered the lists soon after his rejection by the most distinguished family in the place, had been refused. But the chevalier believed that his rival had still such strong chances of success that he dealt him this coup de Jarnac with a blade (namely, Suzanne) that was finely tempered for the purpose. The chevalier had cast his plummet-line into the waters of du Bousquier; and, as we shall see by the sequel, he was not mistaken in any of his conjectures.

Suzanne tripped with a light foot from the rue du Cours, by the rue de la Porte de Seez and the rue du Bercail, to the rue du Cygne, where, about five years earlier, du Bousquier had bought a little house built of gray Jura stone, which is something between Breton slate and Norman granite. There he established himself more comfortably than any householder in town; for he had managed to preserve certain furniture and decorations from the days of his splendor. But provincial manners and morals obscured, little by little, the rays of this fallen Sardanapalus; these vestiges of his former luxury now produced the effect of a glass chandelier in a barn. Harmony, that bond of all work, human or divine, was lacking in great things as well as in little ones. The stairs, up which everybody mounted without wiping their feet, were never polished; the walls, painted by some wretched artisan of the neighborhood, were a terror to the eye; the stone mantel-piece, ill-carved, "swore" with the handsome clock, which was further degraded by the company of contemptible candlesticks. Like the period which du Bousquier himself represented, the house was a jumble of dirt and magnificence. Being considered a man of leisure, du Bousquier led the same parasite life as the chevalier; and he who does not spend his income is always rich. His only servant was a sort of Jocrisse, a lad of the neighborhood, rather a ninny, trained slowly and with difficulty to du Bousquier's requirements. His master had taught him, as he might an orang-outang, to rub the floors, dust the furniture, black his boots, brush his coats, and bring a lantern to guide him home at night if the weather were cloudy, and clogs if it rained. Like many other human beings, this lad hadn't stuff enough in him for more than one vice; he was a glutton. Often, when du Bousquier went to a grand dinner, he would take Rene to wait at table; on such occasions he made him take off his blue cotton jacket, with its big pockets hanging round his hips, and always bulging with handkerchiefs, clasp-knives, fruits, or a handful of nuts, and forced him to put on a regulation coat. Rene would then stuff his fill with the other servants. This duty, which du Bousquier had turned into a reward, won him the most absolute discretion from the Breton servant.

"You here, mademoiselle!" said Rene to Suzanne when she entered; "t'isn't your day. We haven't any linen for the wash, tell Madame Lardot."

"Old stupid!" said Suzanne, laughing.

The pretty girl went upstairs, leaving Rene to finish his porringer of buckwheat in boiled milk. Du Bousquier, still in bed, was revolving in his mind his plans of fortune; for ambition was all that was left to him, as to other men who have sucked dry the orange of pleasure.

Ambition and play are inexhaustible; in a well-organized man the passions which proceed from the brain will always survive the passions of the heart.

"Here am I," said Suzanne, sitting down on the bed and jangling the curtain-rings back along the rod with despotic vehemence.

"Quesaco, my charmer?" said the old bachelor, sitting up in bed.

"Monsieur," said Suzanne, gravely, "you must be astonished to see me here at this hour; but I find myself in a condition which obliges me not to care for what people may say about it."

"What does all that mean?" said du Bousquier, crossing his arms.

"Don't you understand me?" said Suzanne. "I know," she continued, making a pretty little face, "how ridiculous it is in a poor girl to come and nag at a man for what he thinks a mere nothing. But if you really knew me, monsieur, if you knew all that I am capable of for a man who would attach himself to me as much as I'm attached to you, you would never repent having married me. Of course it isn't here, in Alencon, that I should be of service to you; but if we went to Paris, you would see where I could lead a man with your mind and your capacities; and just at this time too, when they are remaking the government from top to toe. So - between ourselves, be it said - *is* what has happened a misfortune? Isn't it rather a piece of luck, which will pay you well? Who and what are you working for now?"

"For myself, of course!" cried du Bousquier, brutally.

"Monster! you'll never be a father!" said Suzanne, giving a tone of prophetic malediction to the words.

"Come, don't talk nonsense, Suzanne," replied du Bousquier; "I really think I am still dreaming."

"How much more reality do you want?" cried Suzanne, standing up.

Du Bousquier rubbed his cotton night-cap to the top of his head with a rotatory motion, which plainly indicated the tremendous fermentation of his ideas.

"He actually believes it!" thought Suzanne, "and he's flattered. Heaven! how easy it is to gull men!"

"Suzanne, what the devil must I do? It is so extraordinary - I, who thought - The fact is that - No, no, it can't be -"

"What? you can't marry me?"

"Oh! as for that, no; I have engagements."

"With Mademoiselle Armande or Mademoiselle Cormon, who have both refused you? Listen to me, Monsieur du Bousquier, my honor doesn't need gendarmes to drag you to the mayor's office. I sha'n't lack for husbands, thank goodness! and I don't want a man who can't appreciate what I'm worth. But some day you'll repent of the way you are behaving; for I tell you now that nothing on earth, neither gold nor silver, will induce me to return the good thing that belongs to you, if you refuse to accept it to-day."

"But, Suzanne, are you sure?"

"Oh, monsieur!" cried the grisette, wrapping her virtue round her, "what do you take me for? I don't remind you of the promises you made me, which have ruined a poor young girl whose only blame was to have as much ambition as love."

Du Bousquier was torn with conflicting sentiments, joy, distrust, calculation. He had long determined to marry Mademoiselle Cormon; for the Charter, on which he had just been ruminating, offered to his ambition, through the half of her property, the political career of a deputy. Besides, his marriage with the old maid would put him socially so high in the town that he would have great influence. Consequently, the storm upraised by that malicious Suzanne drove him into the wildest embarrassment. Without this secret scheme, he would have married Suzanne without hesitation. In which case, he could openly assume the leadership of the liberal party in Alencon. After such a marriage he would, of course, renounce the best society and take up with the bourgeois class of trades-men, rich manufacturers and graziers, who would certainly carry him in triumph as their candidate. Du Bousquier already foresaw the Left side.

This solemn deliberation he did not conceal; he rubbed his hands over his head, displacing the cap which covered its disastrous baldness. Suzanne, meantime, like all those persons who succeed beyond their hopes, was silent and amazed. To hide her astonishment, she assumed the melancholy pose of an injured girl at the mercy of her seducer; inwardly she was laughing like a grisette at her clever trick.

"My dear child," said du Bousquier at length, "I'm not to be taken in with such *bosh*, not I!"

Such was the curt remark which ended du Bousquier's meditation. He plumed himself on belonging to the class of cynical philosophers who could never be "taken in" by women, - putting them, one and all, unto the same category, as *suspicious*. These strong-minded persons are usually weak men who have a special catechism in the matter of womenkind. To them the whole sex, from queens of France to milliners, are essentially depraved, licentious, intriguing, not a little rascally, fundamentally deceitful, and incapable of thought about anything but trifles. To them, women are evil-doing queens, who must be allowed to dance and sing and laugh as they please; they see nothing sacred or saintly in them, nor anything grand; to them there is no poetry in the senses, only gross sensuality. Where such jurisprudence prevails, if a woman is not perpetually tyrannized over, she reduces the man to the condition of a slave. Under this aspect du Bousquier was again the antithesis of the chevalier. When he made his final remark, he flung his night-cap to the foot of the bed, as Pope Gregory did the taper when he fulminated an excommunication; Suzanne then learned for the first time that du Bousquier wore a toupet covering his bald spot.

"Please to remember, Monsieur du Bousquier," she replied majestically, "that in coming here to tell you of this matter I have done my duty; remember that I have offered you my hand, and asked for yours; but remember also that I behaved with the dignity of a woman who respects herself. I have not abased myself to weep like a silly fool; I have not insisted; I have not tormented you. You now know my situation. You must see that I cannot stay in Alencon: my mother would beat me, and Madame Lardot rides a hobby of principles; she'll turn me off. Poor work-girl that I am, must I go to the hospital? must I beg my bread? No! I'd rather throw myself into the Brillante or the Sarthe. But isn't it better that I should go to Paris? My mother could find an excuse to send me there, - an uncle who wants me, or a dying aunt, or a lady who sends for me. But I must have some money for the journey and for - you know what."

This extraordinary piece of news was far more startling to du Bousquier than to the Chevalier de Valois. Suzanne's fiction introduced such confusion into the ideas of the old bachelor that he was literally incapable of sober reflection. Without this agitation and without his inward delight (for vanity is a swindler which never fails of its dupe), he would certainly have reflected that, supposing it were true, a girl like Suzanne, whose heart was not yet spoiled, would have died a thousand deaths before beginning a discussion of this kind and asking for money.

"Will you really go to Paris, then?" he said.

A flash of gayety lighted Suzanne's gray eyes as she heard these words; but the self-satisfied du Bousquier saw nothing.

"Yes, monsieur," she said.

Du Bousquier then began bitter lamentations: he had the last payments to make on his house; the painter, the mason, the upholsterers must be paid. Suzanne let him run on; she was listening for the figures. Du Bousquier offered her three hundred francs. Suzanne made what is called on the stage a false exit; that is, she marched toward the door.

"Stop, stop! where are you going?" said du Bousquier, uneasily. "This is what comes of a bachelor's life!" thought he. "The devil take me if I ever did anything more than rumple her collar, and, lo and behold! she makes THAT a ground to put her hand in one's pocket!"

"I'm going, monsieur," replied Suzanne, "to Madame Granson, the treasurer of the Maternity Society, who, to my knowledge, has saved many a poor girl in my condition from suicide."

"Madame Granson!"

"Yes," said Suzanne, "a relation of Mademoiselle Cormon, the president of the Maternity Society. Saving your presence, the ladies of the town have created an institution to protect poor creatures from destroying their infants, like that handsome Faustine of Argentan who was executed for it three years ago."

"Here, Suzanne," said du Bousquier, giving her a key, "open that secretary, and take out the bag you'll find there: there's about six hundred francs in it; it is all I possess."

"Old cheat!" thought Suzanne, doing as he told her, "I'll tell about your false toupet."

She compared du Bousquier with that charming chevalier, who had given her nothing, it is true, but who had comprehended her, advised her, and carried all grisettes in his heart.

"If you deceive me, Suzanne," cried du Bousquier, as he saw her with her hand in the drawer, "you -"

"Monsieur," she said, interrupting him with ineffable impertinence, "wouldn't you have given me money if I had asked for it?"

Recalled to a sense of gallantry, du Bousquier had a remembrance of past happiness and grunted his assent. Suzanne took the bag and departed, after allowing the old bachelor to kiss her, which he did with an air that seemed to say, "It is a right which costs me dear; but it is better than being harried by a lawyer in the court of assizes as the seducer of a girl accused of infanticide."

Suzanne hid the sack in a sort of gamebag made of osier which she had on her arm, all the while cursing du Bousquier for his stinginess; for one thousand francs was the sum she wanted. Once tempted of the devil to desire that sum, a girl will go far when she has set foot on the path of trickery. As she made her way along the rue du Bercail, it came into her head that the Maternity Society, presided over by Mademoiselle Cormon, might be induced to complete the sum at which she had reckoned her journey to Paris, which to a grisette of Alencon seemed considerable. Besides, she hated du Bousquier. The latter had evidently feared a revelation of his supposed misconduct to Madame Granson; and Suzanne, at the risk of not getting a penny from the society, was possessed with the desire, on leaving Alencon, of entangling the old bachelor in the inextricable meshes of a provincial slander. In all grisettes there is something of the malevolent mischief of a monkey. Accordingly, Suzanne now went to see Madame Granson, composing her face to an expression of the deepest dejection.

Honore de Balzac

CHAPTER III

ATHANASE

Madame Granson, widow of a lieutenant-colonel of artillery killed at Jena, possessed, as her whole means of livelihood, a meagre pension of nine hundred francs a year, and three hundred francs from property of her own, plus a son whose support and education had eaten up all her savings. She occupied, in the rue du Bercail, one of those melancholy ground-floor apartments which a traveller passing along the principal street of a little provincial town can look through at a glance. The street door opened at the top of three steep steps; a passage led to an interior courtyard, at the end of which was the staircase covered by a wooden gallery. On one side of the passage was the dining-room and the kitchen; on the other side, a salon put to many uses, and the widow's bedchamber.

Athanase Granson, a young man twenty-three years of age, who slept in an attic room above the second floor of the house, added six hundred francs to the income of his poor mother, by the salary of a little place which the influence of his relation, Mademoiselle Cormon, had obtained for him in the mayor's office, where he was placed in charge of the archives.

From these indications it is easy to imagine Madame

Granson in her cold salon with its yellow curtains and Utrecht velvet furniture, also yellow, as she straightened the round straw mats which were placed before each chair, that visitors might not soil the red-tiled floor while they sat there; after which she returned to her cushioned armchair and little work-table placed beneath the portrait of the lieutenant-colonel of artillery between two windows, - a point from which her eye could rake the rue du Bercail and see all comers. She was a good woman, dressed with bourgeois simplicity in keeping with her wan face furrowed by grief. The rigorous humbleness of poverty made itself felt in all the accessories of this household, the very air of which was charged with the stern and upright morals of the provinces. At this moment the son and mother were together in the dining-room, where they were breakfasting with a cup of coffee, with bread and butter and radishes. To make the pleasure which Suzanne's visit was to give to Madame Granson intelligible, we must explain certain secret interests of the mother and son.

Athanase Granson was a thin and pale young man, of medium height, with a hollow face in which his two black eyes, sparkling with thoughts, gave the effect of bits of coal. The rather irregular lines of his face, the curve of his lips, a prominent chin, the fine modelling of his forehead, his melancholy countenance, caused by a sense of his poverty warring with the powers that he felt within him, were all indications of repressed and imprisoned talent. In any other place than the town of Alencon the mere aspect of his person would have won him the assistance of superior men, or of women who are able to recognize genius in obscurity. If his was not genius, it was at any rate the form and aspect of it; if he had not the actual force of a great heart, the glow of such a heart was in his glance. Although he was capable of expressing the highest feeling, a casing of timidity destroyed all the graces of his youth, just as the ice of poverty kept him from daring to put forth all his powers. Provincial life, without an opening, without appreciation, without encouragement, described a circle about him in which languished and died the power of thought, - a power which as yet had scarcely reached its dawn. Moreover, Athanase possessed that savage pride which poverty intensifies in noble minds, exalting them in their struggle with men and things; although at their start in life it is an obstacle to their advancement. Genius proceeds in two ways: either it takes its opportunity - like Napoleon, like Moliere - the moment that it sees it, or it waits to be sought when it has patiently revealed itself. Young Granson belonged to that class of men of talent who distrust themselves and are easily discouraged. His soul was contemplative. He lived more by thought than by action. Perhaps he might have seemed deficient or incomplete to those who cannot conceive of genius without the sparkle of French passion; but he was powerful in the world of mind, and he was liable to reach, through a series of emotions imperceptible to common souls, those sudden determinations which make fools say of a man, "He is mad."

The contempt which the world pours out on poverty was death to Athanase; the enervating heat of solitude, without a breath or current of air, relaxed the bow which ever strove to tighten itself; his soul grew weary in this painful effort without results. Athanase was a man who might have taken his place among the glories of France; but, eagle as he was, cooped in a cage without his proper nourishment, he was about to die of hunger after contemplating with an ardent eye the fields of air and the mountain heights where genius soars. His work in the city library escaped attention, and he buried in his soul his thoughts of fame, fearing that they might injure him; but deeper than all lay buried within him the secret of his heart, - a passion which hollowed his cheeks and yellowed his brow. He loved his distant cousin, this very Mademoiselle Cormon whom the Chevalier de Valois and du Bousquier, his hidden rivals, were stalking. This love had had its origin in calculation. Mademoiselle Cormon was thought to be one of the richest persons in the town: the poor lad had therefore been led to love her by desires for material happiness, by the hope, long indulged, of gilding with comfort his mother's last years, by eager longing for the ease of life so needful to men who live by thought; but this most innocent point of departure degraded his passion in his own eyes. Moreover, he feared the ridicule the world would cast upon the love of a young man of twenty-three for an old maid of forty.

And yet his passion was real; whatever may seem false about such a love elsewhere, it can be realized as a fact in the provinces, where, manners and morals being without change or chance or movement or mystery, marriage becomes a necessity of life. No family will accept a young man of dissolute habits. However natural the liaison of a young man, like Athanase, with a handsome girl, like Suzanne, for instance, might seem in a capital, it alarms provincial parents, and destroys the hopes of marriage of a poor young man when possibly the fortune of a rich one might cause such an unfortunate antecedent to be overlooked. Between the depravity of certain liaisons and a sincere love, a man of honor and no fortune will not hesitate: he prefers the misfortunes of virtue to the evils of vice.

But in the provinces women with whom a young man call fall in love are rare. A rich young girl he cannot obtain in a region where all is calculation; a poor young girl he is prevented from loving; it would be, as provincials say, marrying hunger and thirst. Such monkish solitude is, however, dangerous to youth.

These reflections explain why provincial life is so firmly based on marriage. Thus we find that ardent and vigorous genius, forced to rely on the independence of its own poverty, quits these cold regions where thought is persecuted by brutal indifference, where no woman is willing to be a sister of charity to a man of talent, of art, of science.

Who will really understand Athanase Granson's love for Mademoiselle Cormon? Certainly neither rich men - those sultans of society who fill their harems - nor middle-class men, who follow the well-beaten high-road of prejudices; nor women who, not choosing to understand the passions of artists, impose the yoke of their virtues upon men of genius, imagining that the two sexes are governed by the same laws.

Here, perhaps, we should appeal to those young men who suffer from the repression of their first desires at the moment when all their forces are developing; to artists sick of their own genius smothering under the pressure of poverty; to men of talent, persecuted and without influence, often without friends at the start, who have ended by triumphing over that double anguish, equally agonizing, of soul and body. Such men will well understand the lancinating pains of the cancer which was now consuming Athanase; they have gone through those long and bitter deliberations made in presence of some grandiose purpose they had not the means to carry out; they have endured those secret miscarriages in which the fructifying seed of genius falls on arid soil. Such men know that the grandeur of desires is in proportion to the height and breadth of the imagination. The higher they spring, the lower they fall; and how can it be that ties and bonds should not be broken by such a fall? Their piercing eye has seen - as did Athanase - the brilliant future which awaited them, and from which they fancied that only a thin gauze parted them; but that gauze through which their eyes could see is changed by Society into a wall of iron. Impelled by a vocation, by a sentiment of art, they endeavor again and again to live by sentiments which society as incessantly materializes. Alas! the provinces calculate and arrange marriage with the one view of material comfort, and a poor artist or man of science is forbidden to double its purpose and make it the saviour of his genius by securing to him the means of subsistence!

Moved by such ideas, Athanase Granson first thought of marriage with Mademoiselle Cormon as a means of obtaining a livelihood which would be permanent. Thence he could rise to fame, and make his mother happy, knowing at the same time that he was capable of faithfully loving his wife. But soon his own will created, although he did not know it, a genuine passion. He began to study the old maid, and, by dint of the charm which habit gives, he ended by seeing only her beauties and ignoring her defects.

In a young man of twenty-three the senses count for much in love; their fire produces a sort of prism between his eyes and the woman. From this point of view the clasp with which Beaumarchis' Cherubin seizes Marceline is a stroke of genius. But when we reflect that in the utter isolation to which poverty condemned poor Athanase, Mademoiselle Cormon was the only figure presented to his gaze, that she attracted his eye incessantly, that all the light he had was concentrated on her, surely his love may be considered natural.

This sentiment, so carefully hidden, increased from day to day. Desires, sufferings, hopes, and meditations swelled in quietness and silence the lake widening ever in the young man's breast, as hour by hour added its drop of water to the volume. And the wider this inward circle, drawn by the imagination, aided by the senses, grew, the more imposing Mademoiselle Cormon appeared to Athanase, and the more his own timidity increased.

The mother had divined the truth. Like all provincial mothers, she calculated candidly in her own mind the advantages of the match. She told herself that Mademoiselle Cormon would be very lucky to secure a husband in a young man of twenty-three, full of talent, who would always be an honor to his family and the neighborhood; at the same time the obstacles which her son's want of fortune and Mademoiselle Cormon's age presented to the marriage seemed to her almost insurmountable; she could think of nothing but patience as being able to vanquish them. Like du Bousquier, like the Chevalier de Valois, she had a policy of her own; she was on the watch for circumstances, awaiting the propitious moment for a move with the shrewdness of maternal instinct. Madame Granson had no fears at all as to the chevalier, but she did suppose that du Bousquier, although refused, retained certain hopes. As an able and underhand enemy to the latter, she did him much secret harm in the interests of her son; from whom, by the bye, she carefully concealed all such proceedings.

After this explanation it is easy to understand the importance which Suzanne's lie, confided to Madame Granson, was about to acquire. What a weapon put into the hands of this charitable lady, the treasurer of the Maternity Society! How she would gently and demurely spread the news while collecting assistance for the chaste Suzanne!

At the present moment Athanase, leaning pensively on his elbow at the breakfast table, was twirling his spoon in his empty cup and contemplating with a preoccupied eye the poor room with its red brick floor, its straw chairs, its painted wooden buffet, its pink and white curtains chequered like a backgammon board, which communicated with the kitchen through a glass door. As his back was to the chimney which his mother faced, and as the chimney was opposite to the door, his pallid face, strongly lighted from the window, framed in beautiful black hair, the eyes gleaming with despair and fiery with morning thoughts, was the first object which met the eyes of the incoming Suzanne. The grisette, who belonged to a class which certainly has the instinct of misery and the sufferings of the heart, suddenly felt that electric spark, darting from Heaven knows where, which can never be explained, which some strong minds deny, but the sympathetic stroke of which has been felt by many men and many women. It is at once a light which lightens the darkness of the future, a presentiment of the sacred joys of a shared love, the certainty of mutual comprehension. Above all, it is like the touch of a firm and able hand on the keyboard of the senses. The eyes are fascinated by an irresistible attraction; the heart is stirred; the melodies of happiness echo in the soul and in the ears; a voice cries out, "It is he!" Often reflection casts a douche of cold water on this boiling emotion, and all is over.

In a moment, as rapid as the flash of the lightning, Suzanne received the broadside of this emotion in her heart. The flame of a real love burned up the evil weeds fostered by a libertine and dissipated life. She saw how much she was losing of decency and value by accusing herself falsely. What had seemed to her a joke the night before became to her eyes a serious charge against herself. She recoiled at her own success. But the impossibility of any result; the poverty of the young man; a vague hope of enriching herself, of going to Paris, and returning with full hands to say, "I love you! here are the means of happiness!" or mere fate, if you will have it so, dried up the next moment this beneficent dew.

The ambitious grisette asked with a timid air for a moment's interview with Madame Granson, who took her at once into her bedchamber. When Suzanne came out she looked again at Athanase; he was still in the same position, and the tears came into her eyes. As for Madame Granson, she was radiant with joy. At last she had a weapon, and a terrible one, against du Bousquier; she could now deal him a mortal blow. She had of course promised the poor seduced girl the support of all charitable ladies and that of the members of the Maternity Society in particular; she foresaw a dozen visits which would occupy her whole day, and brew up a frightful storm on the head of the guilty du Bousquier. The Chevalier de Valois, while foreseeing the turn the affair would take, had really no idea of the scandal which would result from his own action.

"My dear child," said Madame Granson to her son, "we are to dine, you know, with Mademoiselle Cormon; do take a little pains with your appearance. You are wrong to neglect your dress as you do. Put on that handsome frilled shirt and your green coat of Elbeuf cloth. I have my reasons," she added slyly. "Besides, Mademoiselle Cormon is going to Prebaudet, and many persons will doubtless call to bid her good-bye. When a young man is marriageable he ought to take every means to make himself agreeable. If girls would only tell the truth, heavens! my dear boy, you'd be astonished at what makes them fall in love. Often it suffices for a man to ride past them at the head of a company of artillery, or show himself at a ball in tight clothes. Sometimes a mere turn of the head, a melancholy attitude, makes them suppose a man's whole life; they'll invent a romance to match the hero - who is often a mere brute, but the marriage is made. Watch the Chevalier de Valois: study him; copy his manners; see with what ease he presents himself; he never puts on a stiff air, as you do. Talk a little more; one would really think you didn't know anything, - you, who know Hebrew by heart."

Athanase listened to his mother with a surprised but submissive air; then he rose, took his cap, and went off to the mayor's office, saying to himself, "Can my mother suspect my secret?"

He passed through the rue du Val-Noble, where Mademoiselle Cormon lived, - a little pleasure which he gave himself every morning, thinking, as usual, a variety of fanciful things: -

"How little she knows that a young man is passing before her house who loves her well, who would be faithful to her, who would never cause her any grief; who would leave her the entire management of her fortune without interference. Good God! what fatality! here, side by side, in the same town, are two persons in our mutual condition, and yet nothing can bring them together. Suppose I were to speak to her this evening?"

During this time Suzanne had returned to her mother's house thinking of Athanase; and, like many other women who have longed to help an adored man beyond the limit of human powers, she felt herself capable of making her body a stepping-stone on which he could rise to attain his throne.

It is now necessary to enter the house of this old maid toward whom so many interests are converging, where the actors in this scene, with the exception of Suzanne, were all to meet this very evening. As for Suzanne, that handsome individual bold enough to burn her ships like Alexander at her start in life, and to begin the battle by a falsehood, she disappears from the stage, having introduced upon it a violent element of interest. Her utmost wishes were gratified. She quitted her native town a few days later, well supplied with money and good clothes, among which was a fine dress of green reps and a charming green bonnet lined with pink, the gift of Monsieur de Valois, - a present which she preferred to all the rest, even the money. If the chevalier had gone to Paris in the days of her future brilliancy, she would certainly have left every one for him. Like the chaste Susannah of the Bible, whom the Elders hardly saw, she established herself joyously and full of hope in Paris, while all Alencon was deploring her misfortunes, for which the ladies of two Societies (Charity and Maternity) manifested the liveliest sympathy. Though Suzanne is a fair specimen of those handsome Norman women whom a learned physician reckons as comprising one third of her fallen class whom our monstrous Paris absorbs, it must be stated that she remained in the upper and more decent regions of gallantry. At an epoch when, as Monsieur de Valois said, Woman no longer existed, she was simply "Madame du Val-Noble"; in other days she would have rivalled the Rhodopes, the Imperias, the Ninons of the past. One of the most distinguished writers of the Restoration has taken her under his protection; perhaps he may marry her. He is a journalist, and consequently above public opinion, inasmuch as he manufactures it afresh every year or two.

CHAPTER IV

MADEMOISELLE CORMON

In nearly all the second-class prefectures of France there exists one salon which is the meeting-ground of those considerable and well-considered persons of the community who are, nevertheless, *not* the cream of the best society. The master and mistress of such an establishment are counted among the leading persons of the town; they are received wherever it may please them to visit; no fete is given, no formal or diplomatic dinner takes place, to which they are not invited. But the chateau people, heads of families possessing great estates, in short, the highest personages in the department, do not go to their houses; social intercourse between them is carried on by cards from one to the other, and a dinner or soiree accepted and returned.

This salon, in which the lesser nobility, the clergy, and the magistracy meet together, exerts a great influence. The judgment and mind of the region reside in that solid, unostentatious society, where each man knows the resources of his neighbor, where complete indifference is shown to luxury and dress, - pleasures which are thought childish in comparison to that of obtaining ten or twelve acres of pasture land, - a purchase coveted for years, which has probably given rise to endless diplomatic combinations. Immovable in its prejudices, good or evil, this social circle follows a beaten track, looking neither before it nor behind it. It accepts nothing from Paris without long examination and trial; it rejects cashmeres as it does investments on the Grand-Livre; it scoffs at fashions and novelties; reads nothing, prefers ignorance, whether of science, literature, or industrial inventions. It insists on the removal of a prefect when that official does not suit it; and if the administration resists, it isolates him, after the manner of bees who wall up a snail in wax when it gets into their hive.

In this society gossip is often turned into solemn verdicts. Young women are seldom seen there; when they come it is to seek approbation of their conduct, - a consecration of their self-importance. This supremacy granted to one house is apt to wound the sensibilities of other natives of the region, who console themselves by adding up the cost it involves, and by which they profit. If it so happens that there is no fortune large enough to keep open house in this way, the big-wigs of the place choose a place of meeting, as they did at Alencon, in the house of some inoffensive person, whose settled life and character and position offers no umbrage to the vanities or the interests of any one.

For some years the upper classes of Alencon had met in this way at the house of an old maid, whose fortune was, unknown to herself, the aim and object of Madame Granson, her second cousin, and of the two old bachelors whose secret hopes in that direction we have just unveiled. This lady lived with her maternal uncle, a former grand-vicar of the bishopric of Seez, once her guardian, and whose heir she was. The family of which Rose-Marie-Victoire Cormon was the present representative had been in earlier days among the most considerable in the province. Though belonging to the middle classes, she consorted with the nobility, among whom she was more or less allied, her family having furnished, in past years, stewards to the Duc d'Alencon, many magistrates to the long robe, and various bishops to the clergy. Monsieur de Sponde, the maternal grandfather of Mademoiselle Cormon, was elected by the Nobility to the States-General, and Monsieur Cormon, her father, by the Tiers-Etat, though neither accepted the mission. For the last hundred years the daughters of the family had married nobles belonging to the provinces; consequently, this family had thrown out so many suckers throughout the duchy as to appear on nearly all the genealogical trees. No bourgeois family had ever seemed so like nobility.

The house in which Mademoiselle Cormon lived, build in Henri IV.'s time, by Pierre Cormon, the steward of the last Duc d'Alencon, had always belonged to the family; and among the old maid's visible possessions this one was particularly stimulating to the covetous desires of the two old lovers. Yet, far from producing revenue, the house was a cause of expense. But it is so rare to find in the very centre of a provincial town a private dwelling without unpleasant surroundings, handsome in outward structure and convenient within, that Alencon shared the envy of the lovers.

This old mansion stands exactly in the middle of the rue du Val-Noble. It is remarkable for the strength of its construction, - a style of building introduced by Marie de' Medici. Though built of granite, - a stone which is hard to work, - its angles, and the casings of the doors and windows, are decorated with corner blocks cut into diamond facets. It has only one clear story above the ground-floor; but the roof, rising steeply, has several projecting windows, with carved spandrels rather elegantly enclosed in oaken frames, and externally adorned with balustrades. Between each of these windows is a gargoyle presenting the fantastic jaws of an animal without a body, vomiting the rain-water upon large stones pierced with five holes. The two gables are surmounted by leaden bouquets, - a symbol of the bourgeoisie; for nobles alone had the privilege in former days of having weather-vanes. To right of the courtyard are the stables and coach-house; to left, the kitchen, wood-house, and laundry.

One side of the porte-cochere, being left open, allowed the passers in the street to see in the midst of the vast courtyard a flower-bed, the raised earth of which was held in place by a low privet hedge. A few monthly roses, pinkes, lilies, and Spanish broom filled this bed, around which in the summer season boxes of paurestinus, pomegranates, and myrtle were placed. Struck by the scrupulous cleanliness of the courtyard and its dependencies, a stranger would at once have divined that the place belonged to an old maid. The eye which presided there must have been an unoccupied, ferreting eye; minutely careful, less from nature than for want of something to do. An old maid, forced to employ her vacant days, could alone see to the grass being hoed from between the paving stones, the tops of the walls kept clean, the broom continually going, and the leather curtains of the coach-house always closed. She alone would have introduced, out of busy idleness, a sort of Dutch cleanliness into a house on the confines of Bretagne and Normandie, - a region where they take pride in professing an utter indifference to comfort.

Never did the Chevalier de Valois, or du Bousquier, mount the steps of the double stairway leading to the portico of this house without saying to himself, one, that it was fit for a peer of France, the other, that the mayor of the town ought to live there.

A glass door gave entrance from this portico into an antechamber, a species of gallery paved in red tiles and wainscoted, which served as a hospital for the family portraits, - some having an eye put out, others suffering from a dislocated shoulder; this one held his hat in a hand that no longer existed; that one was a case of amputation at the knee. Here were deposited the cloaks, clogs, overshoes, umbrellas, hoods, and pelisses of the guests. It was an arsenal where each arrival left his baggage on arriving, and took it up when departing. Along each wall was a bench for the servants who arrived with lanterns, and a large stove, to counteract the north wind, which blew through this hall from the garden to the courtyard.

The house was divided in two equal parts. On one side, toward the courtyard, was the well of the staircase, a large dining-room looking to the garden, and an office or pantry which communicated with the kitchen. On the other side was the salon, with four windows, beyond which were two smaller rooms, - one looking on the garden, and used as a boudoir, the other lighted from the courtyard, and used as a sort of office.

The upper floor contained a complete apartment for a family household, and a suite of rooms where the venerable Abbe de Sponde had his abode. The garrets offered fine quarters to the rats and mice, whose nocturnal performances were related by Mademoiselle Cormon to the Chevalier de Valois, with many expressions of surprise at the inutility of her efforts to get rid of them. The garden, about half an acre in size, is margined by the Brillante, so named from the particles of mica which sparkle in its bed elsewhere than in the Val-Noble, where its shallow waters are stained by the dyehouses, and loaded with refuse from the other industries of the town. The shore opposite to Mademoiselle Cormon's garden is crowded with houses where a variety of trades are carried on; happily for her, the occupants are quiet people, - a baker, a cleaner, an upholsterer, and several bourgeois. The garden, full of common flowers, ends in a natural terrace, forming a quay, down which are several steps leading to the river. Imagine on the balustrade of this terrace a number of tall vases of blue and white pottery, in which are gilliflowers; and to right and left, along the neighboring walls, hedges of linden closely trimmed in, and you will gain an idea of the landscape, full of tranquil chastity, modest cheerfulness, but commonplace withal, which surrounded the venerable edifice of the Cormon family. What peace! what tranquillity! nothing pretentious, but nothing transitory; all seems eternal there!

The ground-floor is devoted wholly to the reception-rooms. The old, unchangeable provincial spirit pervades them. The great square salon has four windows, modestly cased in woodwork painted gray. A single oblong mirror is placed above the fireplace; the top of its frame represented the Dawn led by the Hours, and painted in camaieu (two shades of one color). This style of painting infested the decorative art of the day, especially above door-frames, where the artist displayed his eternal Seasons, and made you, in most houses in the centre of France, abhor the odious Cupids, endlessly employed in skating, gleaning, twirling, or garlanding one another with flowers. Each window was draped in green damask curtains, looped up by heavy cords, which made them resemble a vast dais. The furniture, covered with tapestry, the woodwork, painted and varnished, and remarkable for the twisted forms so much the fashion in the last century, bore scenes from the fables of La Fontaine on the chair-backs; some of this tapestry had been mended. The ceiling was divided at the centre of the room by a huge beam, from which depended an old chandelier of rock-crystal swathed in green gauze. On the fireplace were two vases in Sevres blue, and two old girandoles attached to the frame of the mirror, and a clock, the subject of which, taken from the last scene of the "Deserteur," proved the enormous popularity of Sedaine's work. This clock, of bronze-gilt, bore eleven personages upon it, each about four inches tall. At the back the Deserter was seen issuing from prison between the soldiers; in the foreground the young woman lay fainting, and pointing to his pardon. On the walls of this salon were several of the more recent portraits of the family, - one or two by Rigaud, and three pastels by Latour. Four card tables, a backgammon board, and a piquet table occupied the vast room, the only one in the house, by the bye, which was ceiled.

The dining-room, paved in black and white stone, not ceiled, and its beams painted, was furnished with one of those enormous sideboards with marble tops, required by the war waged in the provinces against the human stomach. The walls, painted in fresco, represented a flowery trellis. The seats were of varnished cane, and the doors of natural wood. All things about the place carried out the patriarchal air which emanated from the inside as well as the outside of the house. The genius of the provinces preserved everything; nothing was new or old, neither young nor decrepit. A cold precision made itself felt throughout.

Tourists in Normandy, Brittany, Maine, and Anjou must all have seen in the capitals of those provinces many houses which resemble more or less that of the Cormons; for it is, in its way, an archetype of the burgher houses in that region of France, and it deserves a place in this history because it serves to explain manners and customs, and represents ideas. Who does not already feel that life must have been calm and monotonously regular in this old edifice? It contained a library; but that was placed below the level of the river. The books were well bound and shelved, and the dust, far from injuring them, only made them valuable. They were preserved with the care given in these provinces deprived of vineyards to other native products, desirable for their antique perfume, and issued by the presses of Bourgogne, Touraine, Gascogne, and the South. The cost of transportation was too great to allow any but the best products to be imported.

The basis of Mademoiselle Cormon's society consisted of about one hundred and fifty persons; some went at times to the country; others were occasionally ill; a few travelled about the department on business; but certain of the faithful came every night (unless invited else-where), and so did certain others compelled by duties or by habit to live permanently in the town. All the personages were of ripe age; few among them had ever travelled; nearly all had spent their lives in the provinces, and some had taken part in the chouannerie. The latter were beginning to speak fearlessly of that war, now that rewards were being showered on the defenders of the good cause. Monsieur de Valois, one of the movers in the last uprising (during which the Marquis de Montauran, betrayed by his mistress, perished in spite of the devotion of Marche-a-Terre, now tranquilly raising cattle for the market near Mayenne), - Monsieur de Valois had, during the last six months, given the key to several choice stratagems practised upon an old republican named Hulot, the commander of a demi-brigade stationed at Alencon from 1798 to 1800, who had left many memories in the place. [See "The Chouans."]

The women of this society took little pains with their dress, except on Wednesdays, when Mademoiselle Cormon gave a dinner, on which occasion the guests invited on the previous Wednesday paid their "visit of digestion." Wednesdays were gala days: the assembly was numerous; guests and visitors appeared in fiocchi; some women brought their sewing, knitting, or worsted work; the young girls were not ashamed to make patterns for the Alencon point lace, with the proceeds of which they paid for their personal expenses. Certain husbands brought their wives out of policy, for young men were few in that house; not a word could be whispered in any ear without attracting the attention of all; there was therefore no danger, either for young girls or wives, of love-making.

Every evening, at six o'clock, the long antechamber received its furniture. Each habitue brought his cane, his cloak, his lantern. All these persons knew each other so well, and their habits and ways were so familiarly patriarchal, that if by chance the old Abbe de Sponde was lying down, or Mademoiselle Cormon was in her chamber, neither Josette, the maid, nor Jacquelin, the man-servant, nor Mariette, the cook, informed them. The first comer received the second; then, when the company were sufficiently numerous for whist, piquet, or boston, they began the game without awaiting either the Abbe de Sponde or mademoiselle. If it was dark, Josette or Jacquelin would hasten to light the candles as soon as the first bell rang. Seeing the salon lighted up, the abbe would slowly hurry to come down. Every evening the backgammon and the piquet tables, the three boston tables, and the whist table were filled, - which gave occupation to twenty-five or thirty persons; but as many as forty were usually present. Jacquelin would then light the candles in the other rooms.

Between eight and nine o'clock the servants began to arrive in the antechamber to accompany their masters home; and, short of a revolution, no one remained in the salon at ten o'clock. At that hour the guests were departing in groups along the street, discoursing on the game, or continuing conversations on the land they were covetous of buying, on the terms of some one's will, on quarrels among heirs, on the haughty assumption of the aristocratic portion of the community. It was like Paris when the audience of a theatre disperses.

Certain persons who talk much of poesy and know nothing about it, declaim against the habits of life in the provinces. But put your forehead in your left hand, rest one foot on the fender, and your elbow on your knee; then, if you compass the idea of this quiet and uniform scene, this house and its interior, this company and its interests, heightened by the pettiness of its intellect like goldleaf beaten between sheets of parchment, ask yourself, What is human life? Try to decide between him who scribbles jokes on Egyptian obelisks, and him who has "bostoned" for twenty years with Du Bousquier, Monsieur de Valois, Mademoiselle Cormon, the judge of the court, the king's attorney, the Abbe de Sponde, Madame Granson, and tutti quanti. If

Honore de Balzac

the daily and punctual return of the same steps to the same path is not happiness, it imitates happiness so well that men driven by the storms of an agitated life to reflect upon the blessings of tranquillity would say that here was happiness *enough.*

To reckon the importance of Mademoiselle Cormon's salon at its true value, it will suffice to say that the born statistician of the society, du Bousquier, had estimated that the persons who frequented it controlled one hundred and thirty-one votes in the electoral college, and mustered among themselves eighteen hundred thousand francs a year from landed estate in the neighborhood.

The town of Alencon, however, was not entirely represented by this salon. The higher aristocracy had a salon of their own; moreover, that of the receiver-general was like an administration inn kept by the government, where society danced, plotted, fluttered, loved, and supped. These two salons communicated by means of certain mixed individuals with the house of Cormon, and vice-versa; but the Cormon establishment sat severely in judgment on the two other camps. The luxury of their dinners was criticised; the ices at their balls were pondered; the behavior of the women, the dresses, and "novelties" there produced were discussed and disapproved.

Mademoiselle Cormon, a species of firm, as one might say, under whose name was comprised an imposing coterie, was naturally the aim and object of two ambitious men as deep and wily as the Chevalier de Valois and du Bousquier. To the one as well as to the other, she meant election as deputy, resulting, for the noble, in the peerage, for the purveyor, in a receiver-generalship. A leading salon is a difficult thing to create, whether in Paris or the provinces, and here was one already created. To marry Mademoiselle Cormon was to reign in Alencon. Athanase Granson, the only one of the three suitors for the hand of the old maid who no longer calculated profits, now loved her person as well as her fortune.

To employ the jargon of the day, is there not a singular drama in the situation of these four personages? Surely there is something odd and fantastic in three rivalries silently encompassing a woman who never guessed their existence, in spite of an eager and legitimate desire to be married. And yet, though all these circumstances make the spinsterhood of this old maid an extraordinary thing, it is not difficult to explain how and why, in spite of her fortune and her three lovers, she was still unmarried. In the first place, Mademoiselle Cormon, following the custom and rule of her house, had always desired to marry a nobleman; but from 1788 to 1798 public circumstances were very unfavorable to such pretensions. Though she wanted to be a woman of condition, as the saying is, she was horribly afraid of the Revolutionary tribunal. The two sentiments, equal in force, kept her stationary by a law as true in ethics as it is in statics. This state of uncertain expectation is pleasing to unmarried women as long as they feel themselves young, and in a position to choose a husband. France knows that the political system of Napoleon resulted in making many widows. Under that regime heiresses were entirely out of proportion in numbers to the bachelors who wanted to marry. When the Consulate restored internal order, external difficulties made the marriage of Mademoiselle Cormon as difficult to arrange as it had been in the past. If, on the one hand, Rose-Marie-Victoire refused to marry an old man, on the other, the fear of ridicule forbade her to marry a very young one.

In the provinces, families marry their sons early to escape the conscription. In addition to all this, she was obstinately determined not to marry a soldier: she did not intend to take a man and then give him up to the Emperor; she wanted him for herself alone. With these views, she found it therefore impossible, from 1804 to 1815, to enter the lists with young girls who were rivalling each other for suitable matches.

Besides her predilection for the nobility, Mademoiselle Cormon had another and very excusable mania: that of being loved for herself. You could hardly believe the lengths to which this desire led her. She employed her mind on setting traps for her possible lovers, in order to test their real sentiments. Her nets were so well laid that the luckless suitors were all caught, and succumbed to the test she applied to them without their knowledge. Mademoiselle Cormon did not study them; she watched them. A single word said heedlessly, a joke (that she often was unable to understand), sufficed to make her reject an aspirant as unworthy: this one had neither heart nor delicacy; that one told lies, and was not religious; a third only wanted to coin money under the cloak of marriage; another was not of a nature to make a woman happy; here she suspected hereditary gout; there certain immoral antecedents alarmed her. Like the Church, she required a noble priest at her altar; she even wanted to be married for imaginary ugliness and pretended defects, just as other women wish to be loved for the good qualities they have not, and for imaginary beauties. Mademoiselle Cormon's ambition took its rise in the most delicate and sensitive feminine feeling; she longed to reward a lover by revealing to him a thousand virtues after marriage, as other women then betray the imperfections they have hitherto concealed. But she was ill understood. The noble woman met with none but common souls in whom the reckoning of actual interests was paramount, and who knew nothing of the nobler calculations of sentiment.

The farther she advanced towards that fatal epoch so adroitly called the "second youth," the more her distrust increased. She affected to present herself in the most unfavorable light, and played her part so well that the last wooers hesitated to link their fate to that of a person whose virtuous blind-man's-buff required an amount of penetration that men who want the virtuous ready-made would not bestow upon it. The constant fear of being married for her money rendered her suspicious and uneasy beyond all reason. She turned to the rich men; but the rich are in search of great marriages; she feared the poor men, in whom she denied the disinterestedness she sought so eagerly. After each disappointment in marriage, the poor lady, led to despise mankind, began to see them all in a false light. Her character acquired, necessarily, a secret misanthropy, which threw a tinge of bitterness into her conversation, and some severity into her eyes. Celibacy gave to her manners and habits a certain increasing rigidity; for she endeavored to sanctify herself in despair of fate. Noble vengeance! she was cutting for God the rough diamond rejected by man. Before long public opinion was against her; for society accepts the verdict an independent woman renders on herself by not marrying, either through losing suitors or rejecting them. Everybody supposed that these rejections were founded on secret reasons, always ill interpreted. One said she was deformed; another suggested some hidden fault; but the poor girl was really as pure as a saint, as healthy as an infant, and full of loving kindness; Nature had intended her for all the pleasures, all the joys, and all the fatigues of motherhood.

Mademoiselle Cormon did not possess in her person an obliging auxiliary to her desires. She had no other beauty than that very improperly called la beaute du diable, which consists of a buxom freshness of youth that the devil, theologically speaking, could never have, - though perhaps the expression may be explained by the constant desire that must surely possess him to cool and refresh himself. The feet of the heiress were broad and flat. Her leg, which she often exposed to sight by her manner (be it said without malice) of lifting her gown when it rained, could never have been taken for the leg of a woman. It was sinewy, with a thick projecting calf like a sailor's. A stout waist, the plumpness of a wet-nurse, strong dimpled arms, red hands, were all in keeping with the swelling outlines and the fat whiteness of Norman beauty. Projecting eyes, undecided in color, gave to her face, the rounded outline of which had no dignity, an air of surprise and sheepish simplicity, which was suitable perhaps for an old maid. If Rose had not been, as she was, really innocent, she would have seemed so. An aquiline nose contrasted curiously with the narrowness of her forehead; for it is rare that that form of nose does not carry with it a fine brow. In spite of her thick red lips, a sign of great kindliness, the forehead revealed too great a lack of ideas to allow of the heart being guided by intellect; she was evidently benevolent without grace. How severely we reproach Virtue for its defects, and how full of indulgence we all are for the pleasanter qualities of Vice!

Chestnut hair of extraordinary length gave to Rose Cormon's face a beauty which results from vigor and abundance, - the physical qualities most apparent in her person. In the days of her chief pretensions, Rose affected to hold her head at the three-quarter angle, in order to exhibit a very pretty ear, which detached itself from the blue-veined whiteness of her throat and temples, set off, as it was, by her wealth of hair. Seen thus in a ball-dress, she might have seemed handsome. Her protuberant outlines and her vigorous health did, in fact, draw from the officers of the Empire the approving exclamation, -

"What a fine slip of a girl!"

But, as years rolled on, this plumpness, encouraged by a tranquil, wholesome life, had insensibly so ill spread itself over the whole of Mademoiselle Cormon's body that her primitive proportions were destroyed. At the present moment, no corset could restore a pair of hips to the poor lady, who seemed to have been cast in a single mould. The youthful harmony of her bosom existed no longer; and its excessive amplitude made the spectator fear that if she stooped its heavy masses might topple her over. But nature had provided against this by giving her a natural counterpoise, which rendered needless the deceitful adjunct of a bustle; in Rose Cormon everything was genuine. Her chin, as it doubled, reduced the length of her neck, and hindered the easy carriage of her head. Rose had no wrinkles, but she had folds of flesh; and jesters declared that to save chafing she powdered her skin as they do an infant's.

This ample person offered to a young man full of ardent desires like Athanase an attraction to which he had succumbed. Young imaginations, essentially eager and courageous, like to rove upon these fine living sheets of flesh. Rose was like a plump partridge attracting the knife of a gourmet. Many an elegant deep in debt would very willingly have resigned himself to make the happiness of Mademoiselle Cormon. But, alas! the poor girl was now forty years old. At this period, after vainly seeking to put into her life those interests which make the Woman, and finding herself forced to be still unmarried, she fortified her virtue by stern religious practices. She had recourse to religion, the great consoler of oppressed virginity. A confessor had, for the last three years, directed Mademoiselle Cormon rather stupidly in the path of maceration; he advised the use of scourging, which, if modern medical science is to be believed, produces an effect quite the contrary to that expected by the worthy priest, whose hygienic knowledge was not extensive.

These absurd practices were beginning to shed a monastic tint over the face of Rose Cormon, who now saw with something like despair her white skin assuming the yellow tones which proclaim maturity. A slight down on her upper lip, about the corners, began to spread and darken like a trail of smoke; her temples grew shiny; decadence was beginning! It was authentic in Alencon that Mademoiselle Cormon suffered from rush of blood to the head. She confided her ills to the Chevalier de Valois, enumerating her foot-baths, and consulting him as to refrigerants. On such occasions the shrewd old gentleman would pull out his snuff-box, gaze at the Princess Goritza, and say, by way of conclusion: -

"The right composing draught, my dear lady, is a good

and kind husband."

"But whom can one trust?" she replied.

The chevalier would then brush away the snuff which had settled in the folds of his waistcoat or his paduasoy breeches. To the world at large this gesture would have seemed very natural; but it always gave extreme uneasiness to the poor woman.

The violence of this hope without an object was so great that Rose was afraid to look a man in the face lest he should perceive in her eyes the feelings that filled her soul. By a wilfulness, which was perhaps only the continuation of her earlier methods, though she felt herself attracted toward the men who might still suit her, she was so afraid of being accused of folly that she treated them ungraciously. Most persons in her society, being incapable of appreciating her motives, which were always noble, explained her manner towards her co-celibates as the revenge of a refusal received or expected. When the year 1815 began, Rose had reached that fatal age which she dared not avow. She was forty-two years old. Her desire for marriage then acquired an intensity which bordered on monomania, for she saw plainly that all chance of progeny was about to escape her; and the thing which in her celestial ignorance she desired above all things was the possession of children. Not a person in all Alencon ever attributed to this virtuous woman a single desire for amorous license. She loved, as it were, in bulk without the slightest imagination of love. Rose was a Catholic Agnes, incapable of inventing even one of the wiles of Moliere's Agnes.

For some months past she had counted on chance. The

disbandment of the Imperial troops and the reorganization of the Royal army caused a change in the destination of many officers, who returned, some on half-pay, others with or without a pension, to their native towns, - all having a desire to counteract their luckless fate, and to end their life in a way which might to Rose Cormon be a happy beginning of hers. It would surely be strange if, among those who returned to Alencon or its neighborhood, no brave, honorable, and, above all, sound and healthy officer of suitable age could be found, whose character would be a passport among Bonaparte opinions; or some ci-devant noble who, to regain his lost position, would join the ranks of the royalists. This hope kept Mademoiselle Cormon in heart during the early months of that year. But, alas! all the soldiers who thus returned were either too old or too young; too aggressively Bonapartist, or too dissipated; in short, their several situations were out of keeping with the rank, fortune, and morals of Mademoiselle Cormon, who now grew daily more and more desperate. The poor woman in vain prayed to God to send her a husband with whom she could be piously happy: it was doubtless written above that she should die both virgin and martyr; no man suitable for a husband presented himself. The conversations in her salon every evening kept her informed of the arrival of all strangers in Alencon, and of the facts of their fortunes, rank, and habits. But Alencon is not a town which attracts visitors; it is not on the road to any capital; even sailors, travelling from Brest to Paris, never stop there. The poor woman ended by admitting to herself that she was reduced to the aborigines. Her eye now began to assume a certain savage expression, to which the malicious chevalier responded by a shrewd look as he drew out his snuff-box and gazed at the Princess Goritza. Monsieur de Valois was well aware that in the feminine ethics of love fidelity to a first attachment is considered a pledge for the future.

But Mademoiselle Cormon - we must admit it - was wanting in intellect, and did not understand the snuff-box performance. She redoubled her vigilance against "the evil spirit"; her rigid devotion and fixed principles kept her cruel sufferings hidden among the mysteries of private life. Every evening, after the company had left her, she thought of her lost youth, her faded bloom, the hopes of thwarted nature; and, all the while immolating her passions at the feet of the Cross (like poems condemned to stay in a desk), she resolved firmly that if, by chance, any suitor presented himself, to subject him to no tests, but to accept him at once for whatever he might be. She even went so far as to think of marrying a sub-lieutenant, a man who smoked tobacco, whom she proposed to render, by dint of care and kindness, one of the best men in the world, although he was hampered with debts.

But it was only in the silence of night watches that these fantastic marriages, in which she played the sublime role of guardian angel, took place. The next day, though Josette found her mistress' bed in a tossed and tumbled condition, Mademoiselle Cormon had recovered her dignity, and could only think of a man of forty, a land-owner, well preserved, and a quasi-young man.

The Abbe de Sponde was incapable of giving his niece the slightest aid in her matrimonial manoeuvres. The worthy soul, now seventy years of age, attributed the disasters of the French Revolution to the design of Providence, eager to punish a dissolute Church. He had therefore flung himself into the path, long since abandoned, which anchorites once followed in order to reach heaven: he led an ascetic life without proclaiming it, and without external credit. He hid from the world his works of charity, his continual prayers, his penances; he thought that all priests should have acted thus during the days of wrath and terror, and he preached by example. While presenting to the world a calm and smiling face, he had ended by detaching himself utterly from earthly interests; his mind turned exclusively to sufferers, to the needs of the Church, and to his own salvation. He left the management of his property to his niece, who gave him the income of it, and to whom he paid a slender board in order to spend the surplus in secret alms and gifts to the Church.

All the abbe's affections were concentrated on his niece, who regarded him as a father, but an abstracted father, unable to conceive the agitations of the flesh, and thanking God for maintaining his dear daughter in a state of celibacy; for he had, from his youth up, adopted the principles of Saint John Chrysostom, who wrote that "the virgin state is as far above the marriage state as the angel is above humanity." Accustomed to reverence her uncle, Mademoiselle Cormon dared not initiate him into the desires which filled her soul for a change of state. The worthy man, accustomed, on his side, to the ways of the house, would scarcely have liked the introduction of a husband. Preoccupied by the sufferings he soothed, lost in the depths of prayer, the Abbe de Sponde had periods of abstraction which the habitues of the house regarded as absent-mindedness. In any case, he talked little; but his silence was affable and benevolent. He was a man of great height and spare, with grave and solemn manners, though his face expressed all gentle sentiments and an inward calm;

while his mere presence carried with it a sacred authority. He was very fond of the Voltairean chevalier. Those two majestic relics of the nobility and clergy, though of very different habits and morals, recognized each other by their generous traits. Besides, the chevalier was as unctuous with the abbe as he was paternal with the grisettes.

Some persons may fancy that Mademoiselle Cormon used every means to attain her end; and that among the legitimate lures of womanhood she devoted herself to dress, wore low-necked gowns, and employed the negative coquetries of a magnificent display of arms. Not at all! She was as heroic and immovable in her high-necked chemisette as a sentry in his box. Her gowns, bonnets, and chiffons were all cut and made by the dressmaker and the milliner of Alencon, two hump-backed sisters, who were not without some taste. In spite of the entreaties of these artists, Mademoiselle Cormon refused to employ the airy deceits of elegance; she chose to be substantial in all things, flesh and feathers. But perhaps the heavy fashion of her gowns was best suited to her cast of countenance. Let those laugh who will at this poor girl; you would have thought her sublime, O generous souls! who care but little what form true feeling takes, but admire it where it *is*.

Here some light-minded person may exclaim against the truth of this statement; they will say that there is not in all France a girl so silly as to be ignorant of the art of angling for men; that Mademoiselle Cormon is one of those monstrous exceptions which common-sense should prevent a writer from using as a type; that the most virtuous and also the silliest girl who desires to catch her fish knows well how to bait the hook. But

Honore de Balzac

these criticisms fall before the fact that the noble catholic, apostolic, and Roman religion is still erect in Brittany and in the ancient duchy of Alencon. Faith and piety admit of no subtleties. Mademoiselle Cormon trod the path of salvation, preferring the sorrows of her virginity so cruelly prolonged to the evils of trickery and the sin of a snare. In a woman armed with a scourge virtue could never compromise; consequently both love and self-interest were forced to seek her, and seek her resolutely. And here let us have the courage to make a cruel observation, in days when religion is nothing more than a useful means to some, and a poesy to others. Devotion causes a moral ophthalmia. By some providential grace, it takes from souls on the road to eternity the sight of many little earthly things. In a word, pious persons, devotes, are stupid on various points. This stupidity proves with what force they turn their minds to celestial matters; although the Voltairean Chevalier de Valois declared that it was difficult to decide whether stupid people became naturally pious, or whether piety had the effect of making intelligent young women stupid. But reflect upon this carefully: the purest catholic virtue, with its loving acceptance of all cups, with its pious submission to the will of God, with its belief in the print of the divine finger on the clay of all earthly life, is the mysterious light which glides into the innermost folds of human history, setting them in relief and magnifying them in the eyes of those who still have Faith. Besides, if there be stupidity, why not concern ourselves with the sorrows of stupidity as well as with the sorrows of genius? The former is a social element infinitely more abundant than the latter.

So, then, Mademoiselle Cormon was guilty in the eyes of the world of the divine ignorance of virgins. She was no observer, and her behavior with her suitors proved it. At this very moment, a young girl of sixteen, who had never opened a novel, would have read a hundred chapters of a love story in the eyes of Athanase Granson, where Mademoiselle Cormon saw absolutely nothing. Shy herself, she never suspected shyness in others; she did not recognize in the quavering tones of his speech the force of a sentiment he could not utter. Capable of inventing those refinements of sentimental grandeur which hindered her marriage in her early years, she yet could not recognize them in Athanase. This moral phenomenon will not seem surprising to persons who know that the qualities of the heart are as distinct from those of the mind as the faculties of genius are from the nobility of soul. A perfect, all-rounded man is so rare that Socrates, one of the noblest pearls of humanity, declared (as a phrenologist of that day) that he was born to be a scamp, and a very bad one. A great general may save his country at Zurich, and take commissions from purveyors. A great musician may conceive the sublimest music and commit a forgery. A woman of true feeling may be a fool. In short, a devote may have a sublime soul and yet be unable to recognize the tones of a noble soul beside her. The caprices produced by physical infirmities are equally to be met with in the mental and moral regions.

This good creature, who grieved at making her yearly preserves for no one but her uncle and herself, was becoming almost ridiculous. Those who felt a sympathy for her on account of her good qualities, and others on account of her defects, now made fun of her abortive marriages. More than one conversation was based on what would become of so fine a property, together with the old maid's savings and her uncle's inheritance. For some time past she had been suspected of being au fond, in spite of appearances, an "original." In the provinces it was not permissible to be original: being original means having ideas that are not understood by others; the provinces demand equality of mind as well as equality of manners and customs.

The marriage of Mademoiselle Cormon seemed, after 1804, a thing so problematical that the saying "married like Mademoiselle Cormon" became proverbial in Alencon as applied to ridiculous failures. Surely the sarcastic mood must be an imperative need in France, that so excellent a woman should excite the laughter of Alencon. Not only did she receive the whole society of the place at her house, not only was she charitable, pious, incapable of saying an unkind thing, but she was fully in accord with the spirit of the place and the habits and customs of the inhabitants, who liked her as the symbol of their lives; she was absolutely inlaid into the ways of the provinces; she had never quitted them; she imbibed all their prejudices; she espoused all their interests; she adored them.

In spite of her income of eighteen thousand francs from landed property, a very considerable fortune in the provinces, she lived on a footing with families who were less rich. When she went to her country-place at Prebaudet, she drove there in an old wicker carriole, hung on two straps of white leather, drawn by a wheezy mare, and scarcely protected by two leather curtains rusty with age. This carriole, known to all the town, was cared for by Jacquelin as though it were the finest coupe in all Paris. Mademoiselle valued it; she had used it for twelve years, - a fact to which she called attention with the triumphant joy of happy avarice. Most of the inhabitants of the town were grateful to Mademoiselle Cormon for not humiliating them by the luxury she could have displayed; we may even believe that had she imported a caleche from Paris they would have gossiped more about that than about her various matrimonial failures. The most brilliant equipage would, after all, have only taken her, like the old carriole, to Prebaudet. Now the provinces, which look solely to results, care little about the beauty or elegance of the means, provided they are efficient.

CHAPTER V

AN OLD MAID'S HOUSEHOLD

To complete the picture of the internal habits and ways of this house, it is necessary to group around Mademoiselle Cormon and the Abbe de Sponde Jacquelin, Josette, and Mariette, the cook, who employed themselves in providing for the comfort of uncle and niece.

Jacquelin, a man of forty, short, fat, ruddy, and brown, with a face like a Breton sailor, had been in the service of the house for twenty-two years. He waited at table, groomed the mare, gardened, blacked the abbe's boots, went on errands, chopped the wood, drove the carriole, and fetched the oats, straw, and hay from Prebaudet. He sat in the antechamber during the evening, where he slept like a dormouse. He was in love with Josette, a girl of thirty, whom Mademoiselle would have dismissed had she married him. So the poor fond pair laid by their wages, and loved each other silently, waiting, hoping for mademoiselle's own marriage, as the Jews are waiting for the Messiah. Josette, born between Alencon and Mortagne, was short and plump; her face, which looked like a dirty apricot, was not wanting in sense and character; it was said that she ruled her mistress. Josette and Jacquelin, sure of results, endeavored to hide an inward satisfaction which allows it to be supposed that, as lovers, they had discounted the future. Mariette, the cook, who had been fifteen years in the household, knew how to make all the dishes held in most honor in Alencon.

Perhaps we ought to count for much the fat old Norman brown-bay mare, which drew Mademoiselle Cormon to her country-seat at Prebaudet; for the five inhabitants of the house bore to this animal a maniacal affection. She was called Penelope, and had served the family for eighteen years; but she was kept so carefully and fed with such regularity that mademoiselle and Jacquelin both hoped to use her for ten years longer. This beast was the subject of perpetual talk and occupation; it seemed as if poor Mademoiselle Cormon, having no children on whom her repressed motherly feelings could expend themselves, had turned those sentiments wholly on this most fortunate animal.

The four faithful servants - for Penelope's intelligence raised her to the level of the other good servants; while they, on the other hand, had lowered themselves to the mute, submissive regularity of the beast - went and came daily in the same occupations with the infallible accuracy of mechanism. But, as they said in their idiom, they had eaten their white bread first. Mademoiselle Cormon, like all persons nervously agitated by a fixed idea, became hard to please, and nagging, less by nature than from the need of employing her activity. Having no husband or children to occupy her, she fell back on petty details. She talked for hours about mere nothings, on a dozen napkins marked "Z," placed in the closet before the "O's."

"What can Josette be thinking of?" she exclaimed. "Josette is beginning to neglect things."

Mademoiselle inquired for eight days running whether Penelope had had her oats at two o'clock, because on one occasion Jacquelin was a trifle late. Her narrow imagination spent itself on trifles. A layer of dust forgotten by the feather-duster, a slice of toast ill-made by Mariette, Josette's delay in closing the blinds when the sun came round to fade the colors of the furniture, - all these great little things gave rise to serious quarrels in which mademoiselle grew angry. "Everything was changing," she would cry; "she did not know her own servants; the fact was she spoiled them!" On one occasion Josette gave her the "Journee du Chretien" instead of the "Quinzaine de Paques." The whole town heard of this disaster the same evening. Mademoiselle had been forced to leave the church and return home; and her sudden departure, upsetting the chairs, made people suppose a catastrophe had happened. She was therefore obliged to explain the facts to her friends.

"Josette," she said gently, "such a thing must never happen again."

Mademoiselle Cormon was, without being aware of it, made happier by such little quarrels, which served as cathartics to relieve her bitterness. The soul has its needs, and, like the body, its gymnastics. These uncertainties of temper were accepted by Josette and Jacquelin as changes in the weather are accepted by husbandmen. Those worthy souls remark, "It is fine to-day," or "It rains," without arraigning the heavens. And so when they met in the morning the servants would wonder in what humor mademoiselle would get up, just as a farmer wonders about the mists at dawn.

Mademoiselle Cormon had ended, as it was natural she should end, in contemplating herself only in the infinite pettinesses of her life. Herself and God, her confessor and the weekly wash, her preserves and the church services, and her uncle to care for, absorbed her feeble intellect. To her the atoms of life were magnified by an optic peculiar to persons who are selfish by nature or self-absorbed by some accident. Her perfect health gave alarming meaning to the least little derangement of her digestive organs. She lived under the iron rod of the medical science of our forefathers, and took yearly four precautionary doses, strong enough to have killed Penelope, though they seemed to rejuvenate her mistress. If Josette, when dressing her, chanced to discover a little pimple on the still satiny shoulders of mademoiselle, it became the subject of endless inquiries as to the various alimentary articles of the preceding week. And what a triumph when Josette reminded her mistress of a certain hare that was rather "high," and had doubtless raised that accursed pimple! With what joy they said to each other: "No doubt, no doubt, it *was* the hare!"

"Mariette over-seasoned it," said mademoiselle. "I am always telling her to do so lightly for my uncle and for me; but Mariette has no more memory than -"

"The hare," said Josette.

"Just so," replied Mademoiselle; "she has no more memory than a hare, - a very just remark."

Four times a year, at the beginning of each season, Mademoiselle Cormon went to pass a certain number of days on her estate of Prebaudet. It was now the middle of May, the period at which she wished to see how her apple-trees had "snowed," a saying of that region which expressed the effect produced beneath the trees by the falling of their blossoms. When the circular deposit of these fallen petals resembled a layer of snow the owner of the trees might hope for an abundant supply of cider. While she thus gauged her vats, Mademoiselle Cormon also attended to the repairs which the winter necessitated; she ordered the digging of her flower-beds and her vegetable garden, from which she supplied her table. Every season had its own business. Mademoiselle always gave a dinner of farewell to her intimate friends the day before her departure, although she was certain to see them again within three weeks. It was always a piece of news which echoed through Alencon when Mademoiselle Cormon departed. All her visitors, especially those who had missed a visit, came to bid her good-bye; the salon was thronged, and every one said farewell as though she were starting for Calcutta. The next day the shopkeepers would stand at their doors to see the old carriole pass, and they seemed to be telling one another some news by repeating from shop to shop: -

"So Mademoiselle Cormon is going to Prebaudet!"

Some said: "*Her* bread is baked."

"Hey! my lad," replied the next man. "She's a worthy woman; if money always came into such hands we shouldn't see a beggar in the country."

Another said: "Dear me, I shouldn't be surprised if the vineyards were in bloom; here's Mademoiselle Cormon going to Prebaudet. How happens it she doesn't marry?"

"I'd marry her myself," said a wag; "in fact, the marriage is half-made, for here's one consenting party;

but the other side won't. Pooh! the oven is heating for Monsieur du Bousquier."

"Monsieur du Bousquier! Why, she has refused him."

That evening at all the gatherings it was told gravely: -

"Mademoiselle Cormon has gone."

Or: -

"So you have really let Mademoiselle Cormon go."

The Wednesday chosen by Suzanne to make known her scandal happened to be this farewell Wednesday, - a day on which Mademoiselle Cormon drove Josette distracted on the subject of packing. During the morning, therefore, things had been said and done in the town which lent the utmost interest to this farewell meeting. Madame Granson had gone the round of a dozen houses while the old maid was deliberating on the things she needed for the journey; and the malicious Chevalier de Valois was playing piquet with Mademoiselle Armande, sister of a distinguished old marquis, and the queen of the salon of the aristocrats. If it was not uninteresting to any one to see what figure the seducer would cut that evening, it was all important for the chevalier and Madame Granson to know how Mademoiselle Cormon would take the news in her double capacity of marriageable woman and president of the Maternity Society. As for the innocent du Bousquier, he was taking a walk on the promenade, and beginning to suspect that Suzanne had tricked him; this suspicion confirmed him in his principles as to women.

On gala days the table was laid at Mademoiselle Cormon's about half-past three o'clock. At that period the fashionable people of Alencon dined at four. Under the Empire they still dined as in former times at half-past two; but then they supped! One of the pleasures which Mademoiselle Cormon valued most was (without meaning any malice, although the fact certainly rests on egotism) the unspeakable satisfaction she derived from seeing herself dressed as mistress of the house to receive her guests. When she was thus under arms a ray of hope would glide into the darkness of her heart; a voice told her that nature had not so abundantly provided for her in vain, and that some man, brave and enterprising, would surely present himself. Her desire was refreshed like her person; she contemplated herself in her heavy stuffs with a sort of intoxication, and this satisfaction continued when she descended the stairs to cast her redoubtable eye on the salon, the dinner-table, and the boudoir. She would then walk about with the naive contentment of the rich, - who remember at all moments that they are rich and will never want for anything. She looked at her eternal furniture, her curiosities, her lacquers, and said to herself that all these fine things wanted was a master. After admiring the dining-room, and the oblong dinner-table, on which was spread a snow-white cloth adorned with twenty covers placed at equal distances; after verifying the squadron of bottles she had ordered to be brought up, and which all bore honorable labels; after carefully verifying the names written on little bits of paper in the trembling handwriting of the abbe (the only duty he assumed in the household, and one which gave rise to grave discussions on the place of each guest), - after going through all these preliminary acts mademoiselle went, in her fine clothes, to her uncle, who was accustomed at this, the best hour in the day, to take his walk on the terrace which overlooked the Brillante, where he could listen to the warble of birds which were resting in the coppice, unafraid of either sportsmen or children. At such times of waiting she never joined the Abbe de Sponde without asking him some ridiculous question, in order to draw the old man into a discussion which might serve to amuse him. And her reason was this, - which will serve to complete our picture of this excellent woman's nature: -

Mademoiselle Cormon regarded it as one of her duties to talk; not that she was talkative, for she had unfortunately too few ideas, and did not know enough phrases to converse readily. But she believed she was accomplishing one of the social duties enjoined by religion, which orders us to make ourselves agreeable to our neighbor. This obligation cost her so much that she consulted her director, the Abbe Couturier, upon the subject of this honest but puerile civility. In spite of the humble remark of his penitent, confessing the inward labor of her mind in finding anything to say, the old priest, rigid on the point of discipline, read her a passage from Saint-Francois de Sales on the duties of women in society, which dwelt on the decent gayety of pious Christian women, who were bound to reserve their sternness for themselves, and to be amiable and pleasing in their homes, and see that their neighbors enjoyed themselves. Thus, filled with a sense of duty, and wishing, at all costs, to obey her director, who bade her converse with amenity, the poor soul perspired in her corset when the talk around her languished, so much did she suffer from the effort of emitting ideas in order to revive it. Under such circumstances she would put forth the silliest statements, such as: "No one can be in two places at once - unless it is a little bird," by which she one day roused, and not without success, a discussion on the ubiquity of the apostles, which she was unable to comprehend. Such efforts at conversation won her the appellation of "that good Mademoiselle Cormon," which, from the lips of the beaux esprits of society, means that she was as ignorant as a carp, and rather a poor fool; but many persons of her own calibre took the remark in its literal sense, and answered: -

"Yes; oh yes! Mademoiselle Cormon is an excellent woman."

Sometimes she would put such absurd questions (always for the purpose of fulfilling her duties to society, and making herself agreeable to her guests) that everybody burst out laughing. She asked, for instance, what the government did with the taxes they were always receiving; and why the Bible had not been printed in the days of Jesus Christ, inasmuch as it was written by Moses. Her mental powers were those of the English "country gentleman" who, hearing constant mention of "posterity" in the House of Commons, rose to make the speech that has since become celebrated: "Gentlemen," he said, "I hear much talk in this place about Posterity. I should be glad to know what that power has ever done for England."

Under these circumstances the heroic Chevalier de Valois would bring to the succor of the old maid all the powers of his clever diplomacy, whenever he saw the pitiless smile of wiser heads. The old gentleman, who loved to assist women, turned Mademoiselle Cormon's sayings into wit by sustaining them paradoxically, and he often covered the retreat so well that it seemed as if the good woman had said nothing silly. She asserted very seriously one evening that she did not see any difference between an ox and a bull. The dear chevalier instantly arrested the peals of laughter by asserting that there was only the difference between a sheep and a lamb.

But the Chevalier de Valois served an ungrateful dame, for never did Mademoiselle Cormon comprehend his chivalrous services. Observing that the conversation grew lively, she simply thought that she was not so stupid as she was, - the result being that she settled down into her ignorance with some complacency; she lost her timidity, and acquired a self-possession which gave to her "speeches" something of the solemnity with which the British enunciate their patriotic absurdities, - the self-conceit of stupidity, as it may be called.

As she approached her uncle, on this occasion, with a majestic step, she was ruminating over a question that might draw him from a silence, which always troubled her, for she feared he was dull.

"Uncle," she said, leaning on his arm and clinging to his side (this was one of her fictions; for she said to herself "If I had a husband I should do just so"), - "uncle, if everything here below happens according to the will of God, there must be a reason for everything."

"Certainly," replied the abbe, gravely. The worthy man, who cherished his niece, always allowed her to tear him from his meditations with angelic patience.

"Then if I remain unmarried, - supposing that I do, - God wills it?"

"Yes, my child," replied the abbe.

"And yet, as nothing prevents me from marrying to-morrow if I choose, His will can be destroyed by mine?"

"That would be true if we knew what was really the will of God," replied the former prior of the Sorbonne. "Observe, my daughter, that you put in an *if.*"

The poor woman, who expected to draw her uncle into a matrimonial discussion by an argument ad omni-potentem, was stupefied; but persons of obtuse mind have the terrible logic of children, which consists in turning from answer to question, - a logic that is frequently embarrassing.

"But, uncle, God did not make women intending them not to marry; otherwise they ought all to stay unmarried; if not, they ought all to marry. There's great injustice in the distribution of parts."

"Daughter," said the worthy abbe, "you are blaming the Church, which declares celibacy to be the better way to God."

"But if the Church is right, and all the world were good Catholics, wouldn't the human race come to an end, uncle?"

"You have too much mind, Rose; you don't need so much to be happy."

That remark brought a smile of satisfaction to the lips of the poor woman, and confirmed her in the good opinion she was beginning to acquire about herself. That is how the world, our friends, and our enemies are the accomplices of our defects!

At this moment the conversation was interrupted by the successive arrival of the guests. On these ceremonial days, friendly familiarities were exchanged between the servants of the house and the company. Mariette remarked to the chief-justice as he passed the kitchen: -

"Ah, Monsieur du Ronceret, I've cooked the cauliflowers au gratin expressly for you, for mademoiselle knows how you like them; and she said to me: 'Now don't forget, Mariette, for Monsieur du Ronceret is coming.'"

"That good Mademoiselle Cormon!" ejaculated the chief legal authority of the town. "Mariette, did you steep them in gravy instead of soup-stock? it is much richer."

The chief-justice was not above entering the chamber of council where Mariette held court; he cast the eye of a gastronome around it, and offered the advice of a past master in cookery.

"Good-day, madame," said Josette to Madame Granson, who courted the maid. "Mademoiselle has thought of you, and there's fish for dinner."

As for the Chevalier de Valois, he remarked to Mariette, in the easy tone of a great seigneur who condescends to be familiar: -

"Well, my dear cordon-bleu, to whom I should give the cross of the Legion of honor, is there some little dainty for which I had better reserve myself?"

"Yes, yes, Monsieur de Valois, - a hare sent from

Prebaudet; weighs fourteen pounds."

Du Bousquier was not invited. Mademoiselle Cormon, faithful to the system which we know of, treated that fifty-year-old suitor extremely ill, although she felt inexplicable sentiments towards him in the depths of her heart. She had refused him; yet at times she repented; and a presentiment that she should yet marry him, together with a terror at the idea which prevented her from wishing for the marriage, assailed her. Her mind, stimulated by these feelings, was much occupied by du Bousquier. Without being aware of it, she was influenced by the herculean form of the republican. Madame Granson and the Chevalier de Valois, although they could not explain to themselves Mademoiselle Cormon's inconsistencies, had detected her naive glances in that direction, the meaning of which seemed clear enough to make them both resolve to ruin the hopes of the already rejected purveyor, - hopes which it was evident he still indulged.

Two guests, whose functions excused them, kept the dinner waiting. One was Monsieur du Coudrai, the recorder of mortgages; the other Monsieur Choisnel, former bailiff to the house of Esgrignon, and now the notary of the upper aristocracy, by whom he was received with a distinction due to his virtues; he was also a man of considerable wealth. When the two belated guests arrived, Jacquelin said to them as he saw them about to enter the salon: -

"*They* are all in the garden."

No doubt the assembled stomachs were impatient; for on the appearance of the register of mortgages - who had no defect except that of having married for her money an intolerable old woman, and of perpetrating endless puns, at which he was the first to laugh - the gentle murmur by which such late-comers are welcomed arose. While awaiting the official announcement of dinner, the company were sauntering on the terrace above the river, and gazing at the water-plants, the mosaic of the currents, and the various pretty details of the houses clustering across the river, their old wooden galleries, their mouldering window-frames, their little gardens where clothes were drying, the cabinet-maker's shop, - in short, the many details of a small community to which the vicinity of a river, a weeping willow, flowers, rose-bushes, added a certain grace, making the scene quite worthy of a landscape painter.

The chevalier studied all faces, for he knew that his firebrand had been very successfully introduced into the chief houses of the place. But no one as yet referred openly to the great news of Suzanne and du Bousquier. Provincials possess in the highest degree the art of distilling gossip; the right moment for openly discussing this strange affair had not arrived; it was first necessary that all present should put themselves on record. So the whispers went round from ear to ear:-

"You have heard?"

"Yes."

"Du Bousquier?"

"And that handsome Suzanne."

"Does Mademoiselle Cormon know of it?"

"No."

"Ha!"

This was the *piano* of the scandal; the *rinforzando* would break forth as soon as the first course had been removed. Suddenly Monsieur de Valois's eyes lighted on Madame Granson, arrayed in her green hat with bunches of auriculas, and beaming with evident joy. Was it merely the joy of opening the concert? Though such a piece of news was like a gold mine to work in the monotonous lives of these personages, the observant and distrustful chevalier thought he recognized in the worthy woman a far more extended sentiment; namely, the joy caused by the triumph of self-interest. Instantly he turned to examine Athanase, and detected him in the significant silence of deep meditation. Presently, a look cast by the young man on Mademoiselle Cormon carried to the soul of the chevalier a sudden gleam. That momentary flash of lightning enabled him to read the past.

"Ha! the devil!" he said to himself; "what a checkmate I'm exposed to!"

Monsieur de Valois now approached Mademoiselle Cormon, and offered his arm. The old maid's feeling to the chevalier was that of respectful consideration; and certainly his name, together with the position he occupied among the aristocratic constellations of the department made him the most brilliant ornament of her salon. In her inmost mind Mademoiselle Cormon had wished for the last dozen years to become Madame de Valois. That name was like the branch of a tree, to which the ideas which *swarmed* in her mind about rank, nobility, and the external qualities of a husband had fastened. But, though the Chevalier de Valois was the man chosen by her heart, and mind, and ambition, that elderly ruin, combed and curled like a little Saint-John in a procession, alarmed Mademoiselle Cormon. She saw the gentleman in him, but she could not see a husband. The indifference which the chevalier affected as to marriage, above all, the apparent purity of his morals in a house which abounded in grisettes, did singular harm in her mind to Monsieur de Valois against his expectations. The worthy man, who showed such judgment in the matter of his annuity, was at fault here. Without being herself aware of it, the thoughts of Mademoiselle Cormon on the too virtuous chevalier might be translated thus: -

"What a pity that he isn't a trifle dissipated!"

Observers of the human heart have remarked the leaning of pious women toward scamps; some have expressed surprise at this taste, considering it opposed to Christian virtue. But, in the first place, what nobler destiny can you offer to a virtuous woman than to purify, like charcoal, the muddy waters of vice? How is it some observers fail to see that these noble creatures, obliged by the sternness of their own principles never to infringe on conjugal fidelity, must naturally desire a husband of wider practical experience than their own? The scamps of social life are great men in love. Thus the poor woman groaned in spirit at finding her chosen vessel parted into two pieces. God alone could solder together a Chevalier de Valois and a du Bousquier.

In order to explain the importance of the few words which the chevalier and Mademoiselle Cormon are about to say to each other, it is necessary to reveal two

Honore de Balzac

serious matters which agitated the town, and about which opinions were divided; besides, du Bousquier was mysteriously connected with them.

One concerns the rector of Alencon, who had formerly taken the constitutional oath, and who was now conquering the repugnance of the Catholics by a display of the highest virtues. He was Cheverus on a small scale, and became in time so fully appreciated that when he died the whole town mourned him. Mademoiselle Cormon and the Abbe de Sponde belonged to that "little Church," sublime in its orthodoxy, which was to the court of Rome what the Ultras were to be to Louis XVIII. The abbe, more especially, refused to recognize a Church which had compromised with the constitutionals. The rector was therefore not received in the Cormon household, whose sympathies were all given to the curate of Saint-Leonard, the aristocratic parish of Alencon. Du Bousquier, that fanatic liberal now concealed under the skin of a royalist, knowing how necessary rallying points are to all discontents (which are really at the bottom of all oppositions), had drawn the sympathies of the middle classes around the rector. So much for the first case; the second was this: -

Under the secret inspiration of du Bousquier the idea of building a theatre had dawned on Alencon. The henchmen of the purveyor did not know their Mohammed; and they thought they were ardent in carrying out their own conception. Athanase Granson was one of the warmest partisans for the theatre; and of late he had urged at the mayor's office a cause which all the other young clerks had eagerly adopted.

The chevalier, as we have said, offered his arm to the

old maid for a turn on the terrace. She accepted it, not without thanking him by a happy look for this attention, to which the chevalier replied by motioning toward Athanase with a meaning eye.

"Mademoiselle," he began, "you have so much sense and judgment in social proprieties, and also, you are connected with that young man by certain ties -"

"Distant ones," she said, interrupting him.

"Ought you not," he continued, "to use the influence you have over his mother and over himself by saving him from perdition? He is not very religious, as you know; indeed he approves of the rector; but that is not all; there is something far more serious; isn't he throwing himself headlong into an opposition without considering what influence his present conduct may exert upon his future? He is working for the construction of a theatre. In this affair he is simply the dupe of that disguised republican du Bousquier -"

"Good gracious! Monsieur de Valois," she replied; "his mother is always telling me he has so much mind, and yet he can't say two words; he stands planted before me as mum as a post -"

"Which doesn't think at all!" cried the recorder of mortgages. "I caught your words on the fly. I present my compliments to Monsieur de Valois," he added, bowing to that gentleman with much emphasis.

The chevalier returned the salutation stiffly, and drew Mademoiselle Cormon toward some flower-pots at a little distance, in order to show the interrupter that he did not choose to be spied upon.

"How is it possible," he continued, lowering his voice, and leaning towards Mademoiselle Cormon's ear, "that a young man brought up in those detestable lyceums should have ideas? Only sound morals and noble habits will ever produce great ideas and a true love. It is easy to see by a mere look at him that the poor lad is likely to be imbecile, and come, perhaps, to some sad end. See how pale and haggard he is!"

"His mother declares he works too hard," replied the old maid, innocently. "He sits up late, and for what? reading books and writing! What business ought to require a young man to write at night?"

"It exhausts him," replied the chevalier, trying to bring the old maid's thoughts back to the ground where he hoped to inspire her with horror for her youthful lover. "The morals of those Imperial lyceums are really shocking."

"Oh, yes!" said the ingenuous creature. "They march the pupils about with drums at their head. The masters have no more religion than pagans. And they put the poor lads in uniform, as if they were troops. What ideas!"

"And behold the product!" said the chevalier, motioning to Athanase. "In my day, young men were not so shy of looking at a pretty woman. As for him, he drops his eyes whenever he sees you. That young man frightens me because I am really interested in him. Tell him not to intrigue with the Bonapartists, as he is now doing about that theatre. When all these petty folks cease to ask for it insurrectionally, - which to my mind is the synonym of constitutionally, - the government will build it. Besides which, tell his mother to keep an eye on him."

"Oh, I'm sure she will prevent him from seeing those half-pay, questionable people. I'll talk to her," said Mademoiselle Cormon, "for he might lose his place in the mayor's office; and then what would he and his mother have to live on? It makes me shudder."

As Monsieur de Talleyrand said of his wife, so the chevalier said to himself, looking at Mademoiselle Cormon: -

"Find me another as stupid! Good powers! isn't virtue which drives out intellect vice? But what an adorable wife for a man of my age! What principles! what ignorance!"

Remember that this monologue, addressed to the Princess Goritza, was mentally uttered while he took a pinch of snuff.

Madame Granson had divined that the chevalier was talking about Athanase. Eager to know the result of the conversation, she followed Mademoiselle Cormon, who was now approaching the young man with much dignity. But at this moment Jacquelin appeared to announce that mademoiselle was served. The old maid gave a glance of appeal to the chevalier; but the gallant recorder of mortgages, who was beginning to see in the manners of that gentleman the barrier which the provincial nobles were setting up about this time between themselves and the bourgeoisie, made the most of his chance to cut out Monsieur de Valois. He was close to Mademoiselle Cormon, and promptly offered his arm, which she found herself compelled to accept. The chevalier then darted, out of policy, upon

Madame Granson.

"Mademoiselle Cormon, my dear lady," he said to her, walking slowly after all the other guests, "feels the liveliest interest in your dear Athanase; but I fear it will vanish through his own fault. He is irreligious and liberal; he is agitating this matter of the theatre; he frequents the Bonapartists; he takes the side of that rector. Such conduct may make him lose his place in the mayor's office. You know with what care the government is beginning to weed out such opinions. If your dear Athanase loses his place, where can he find other employment? I advise him not to get himself in bad odor with the administration."

"Monsieur le Chevalier," said the poor frightened mother, "how grateful I am to you! You are right: my son is the tool of a bad set of people; I shall enlighten him."

The chevalier had long since fathomed the nature of Athanase, and recognized in it that unyielding element of republican convictions to which in his youth a young man is willing to sacrifice everything, carried away by the word "liberty," so ill-defined and so little understood, but which to persons disdained by fate is a banner of revolt; and to such, revolt is vengeance. Athanase would certainly persist in that faith, for his opinions were woven in with his artistic sorrows, with his bitter contemplation of the social state. He was ignorant of the fact that at thirty-six years of age, - the period of life when a man has judged men and social interests and relations, - the opinions for which he was ready to sacrifice his future would be modified in him, as they are in all men of real superiority. To remain faithful to the Left side of Alencon was to gain the aversion of Mademoiselle Cormon. There, indeed, the chevalier saw true.

Thus we see that this society, so peaceful in appearance, was internally as agitated as any diplomatic circle, where craft, ability, and passions group themselves around the grave questions of an empire. The guests were now seated at the table laden with the first course, which they ate as provincials eat, without shame at possessing a good appetite, and not as in Paris, where it seems as if jaws gnashed under sumptuary laws, which made it their business to contradict the laws of anatomy. In Paris people eat with their teeth, and trifle with their pleasure; in the provinces things are done naturally, and interest is perhaps rather too much concentrated on the grand and universal means of existence to which God has condemned his creatures.

It was at the end of the first course that Mademoiselle Cormon made the most celebrated of her "speeches"; it was talked about for fully two years, and is still told at the gatherings of the lesser bourgeoisie whenever the topic of her marriage comes up.

The conversation, becoming lively as the penultimate entree was reached, had turned naturally on the affair of the theatre and the constitutionally sworn rector. In the first fervor of royalty, during the year 1816, those who later were called Jesuits were all for the expulsion of the Abbe Francois from his parish. Du Bousquier, suspected by Monsieur de Valois of sustaining the priest and being at the bottom of the theatre intrigues, and on whose back the adroit chevalier would in any case have put those sins with his customary cleverness, was in the dock with no lawyer to defend him.

Athanase, the only guest loyal enough to stand by du Bousquier, had not the nerve to emit his ideas in the presence of those potentates of Alencon, whom in his heart he thought stupid. None but provincial youths now retain a respectful demeanor before men of a certain age, and dare neither to censure nor contradict them. The talk, diminished under the effect of certain delicious ducks dressed with olives, was falling flat. Mademoiselle Cormon, feeling the necessity of maintaining it against her own ducks, attempted to defend du Bousquier, who was being represented as a pernicious fomenter of intrigues, capable of any trickery.

"As for me," she said, "I thought that Monsieur du Bousquier cared chiefly for childish things."

Under existing circumstances the remark had enormous success. Mademoiselle Cormon obtained a great triumph; she brought the nose of the Princess Goritza flat on the table. The chevalier, who little expected such an apt remark from his Dulcinea, was so amazed that he could at first find no words to express his admiration; he applauded noiselessly, as they do at the Opera, tapping his fingers together to imitate applause.

"She is adorably witty," he said to Madame Granson. "I always said that some day she would unmask her batteries."

"In private she is always charming," replied the widow.

"In private, madame, all women have wit," returned the chevalier.

The Homeric laugh thus raised having subsided, Mademoiselle Cormon asked the reason of her success. Then began the *forte* of the gossip. Du Bousquier was depicted as a species of celibate Pere Gigogne, a monster, who for the last fifteen years had kept the Foundling Hospital supplied. His immoral habits were at last revealed! these Parisian saturnalias were the result of them, etc., etc. Conducted by the Chevalier de Valois, a most able leader of an orchestra of this kind, the opening of the *cancan* was magnificent.

"I really don't know," he said, "what should hinder a du Bousquier from marrying a Mademoiselle Suzanne What's-her-name. What *is* her name, do you know? Suzette! Though I have lodgings at Madame Lardot's, I know her girls only by sight. If this Suzette is a tall, fine, saucy girl, with gray eyes, a slim waist, and a pretty foot, whom I have occasionally seen, and whose behavior always seemed to me extremely insolent, she is far superior in manners to du Bousquier. Besides, the girl has the nobility of beauty; from that point of view the marriage would be a poor one for her; she might do better. You know how the Emperor Joseph had the curiosity to see the du Barry at Luciennes. He offered her his arm to walk about, and the poor thing was so surprised at the honor that she hesitated to accept it: 'Beauty is ever a queen,' said the Emperor. And he, you know, was an Austrian-German," added the chevalier. "But I can tell you that Germany, which is thought here very rustic, is a land of noble chivalry and fine manners, especially in Poland and Hungary, where -"

Here the chevalier stopped, fearing to slip into some allusion to his personal happiness; he took out his snuff-box, and confided the rest of his remarks to the princess, who had smiled upon him for thirty-six years and more.

"That speech was rather a delicate one for Louis XV.,"
said du Ronceret.

"But it was, I think, the Emperor Joseph who made it,
and not Louis XV.," remarked Mademoiselle Cormon,
in a correcting tone.

"Mademoiselle," said the chevalier, observing the
malicious glance exchanged between the judge, the
notary, and the recorder, "Madame du Barry was the
Suzanne of Louis XV., - a circumstance well known to
scamps like ourselves, but unsuitable for the knowledge of young ladies. Your ignorance proves you to
be a flawless diamond; historical corruptions do not
enter your mind."

The Abbe de Sponde looked graciously at the
Chevalier de Valois, and nodded his head in sign of his
laudatory approbation.

"Doesn't mademoiselle know history?" asked the
recorder of mortgages.

"If you mix up Louis XV. and this girl Suzanne, how
am I to know history?" replied Mademoiselle Cormon,
angelically, glad to see that the dish of ducks was
empty at last, and the conversation so ready to revive
that all present laughed with their mouths full at her
last remark.

"Poor girl!" said the Abbe de Sponde. "When a great
misfortune happens, charity, which is divine love, and
as blind as pagan love, ought not to look into the
causes of it. Niece, you are president of the Maternity

Society; you must succor that poor girl, who will now find it difficult to marry."

"Poor child!" ejaculated Mademoiselle Cormon.

"Do you suppose du Bousquier would marry her?" asked the judge.

"If he is an honorable man he ought to do so," said Madame Granson; "but really, to tell the truth, my dog has better morals than he -"

"Azor is, however, a good purveyor," said the recorder of mortgages, with the air of saying a witty thing.

At dessert du Bousquier was still the topic of conversation, having given rise to various little jokes which the wine rendered sparkling. Following the example of the recorder, each guest capped his neighbor's joke with another: Du Bousquier was a father, but not a confessor; he was father less; he was father LY; he was not a reverend father; nor yet a conscript-father.

"Nor can he be a foster-father," said the Abbe de Sponde, with a gravity which stopped the laughter.

"Nor a noble father," added the chevalier.

The Church and the nobility descended thus into the arena of puns, without, however, losing their dignity.

"Hush!" exclaimed the recorder of mortgages. "I hear the creaking of du Bousquier's boots."

It usually happens that a man is ignorant of rumors that are afloat about him. A whole town may be talking of his affairs; may calumniate and decry him, but if he has no good friends, he will know nothing about it. Now the innocent du Bousquier was superb in his ignorance. No one had told him as yet of Suzanne's revelations; he therefore appeared very jaunty and slightly conceited when the company, leaving the dining-room, returned to the salon for their coffee; several other guests had meantime assembled for the evening. Mademoiselle Cormon, from a sense of shamefacedness, dared not look at the terrible seducer. She seized upon Athanase, and began to lecture him with the queerest platitudes about royalist politics and religious morality. Not possessing, like the Chevalier de Valois, a snuff-box adorned with a princess, by the help of which he could stand this torrent of silliness, the poor poet listened to the words of her whom he loved with a stupid air, gazing, meanwhile, at her enormous bust, which held itself before him in that still repose which is the attribute of all great masses. His love produced in him a sort of intoxication which changed the shrill voice of the old maid into a soft murmur, and her flat remarks into witty speeches. Love is a maker of false coin, continually changing copper pennies into gold-pieces, and sometimes turning its real gold into copper.

"Well, Athanase, will you promise me?"

This final sentence struck the ear of the absorbed young man like one of those noises which wake us with a bound.

"What, mademoiselle?"

Mademoiselle Cormon rose hastily, and looked at du Bousquier, who at that moment resembled the stout god of Fable which the Republic stamped upon her coins. She walked up to Madame Granson, and said in her ear: -

"My dear friend, you son is an idiot. That lyceum has ruined him," she added, remembering the insistence with which the chevalier had spoken of the evils of education in such schools.

What a catastrophe! Unknown to himself, the luckless Athanase had had an occasion to fling an ember of his own fire upon the pile of brush gathered in the heart of the old maid. Had he listened to her, he might have made her, then and there, perceive his passion; for, in the agitated state of Mademoiselle Cormon's mind, a single word would have sufficed. But that stupid absorption in his own sentiments, which characterizes young and true love, had ruined him, as a child full of life sometimes kills itself out of ignorance.

"What have you been saying to Mademoiselle Cormon?" demanded his mother.

"Nothing."

"Nothing; well, I can explain that," she thought to herself, putting off till the next day all further reflection on the matter, and attaching but little importance to Mademoiselle Cormon's words; for she fully believed that du Bousquier was forever lost in the old maid's esteem after the revelation of that evening.

Soon the four tables were filled with their sixteen players. Four persons were playing piquet, - an expensive game, at which the most money was lost. Monsieur Choisnel, the procureur-du-roi, and two ladies went into the boudoir for a game at back-gammon. The glass lustres were lighted; and then the flower of Mademoiselle Cormon's company gathered before the fireplace, on sofas, and around the tables, and each couple said to her as they arrived, -

"So you are going to-morrow to Prebaudet?"

"Yes, I really must," she replied.

On this occasion the mistress of the house appeared preoccupied. Madame Granson was the first to perceive the quite unnatural state of the old maid's mind, - Mademoiselle Cormon was thinking!

"What are you thinking of, cousin?" she said at last, finding her seated in the boudoir.

"I am thinking," she replied, "of that poor girl. As the president of the Maternity Society, I will give you fifty francs for her."

"Fifty francs!" cried Madame Granson. "But you have never given as much as that."

"But, my dear cousin, it is so natural to have children."

That immoral speech coming from the heart of the old maid staggered the treasurer of the Maternity Society. Du Bousquier had evidently advanced in the estimation of Mademoiselle Cormon.

"Upon my word," said Madame Granson, "du Bousquier is not only a monster, he is a villain. When a man has done a wrong like that, he ought to pay the indemnity. Isn't it his place rather than ours to look after the girl? - who, to tell you the truth, seems to me rather questionable; there are plenty of better men in Alencon than that cynic du Bousquier. A girl must be depraved, indeed, to go after him."

"Cynic! Your son teaches you to talk Latin, my dear, which is wholly incomprehensible. Certainly I don't wish to excuse Monsieur du Bousquier; but pray explain to me why a woman is depraved because she prefers one man to another."

"My dear cousin, suppose you married my son Athanase; nothing could be more natural. He is young and handsome, full of promise, and he will be the glory of Alencon; and yet everybody will exclaim against you: evil tongues will say all sorts of things; jealous women will accuse you of depravity, - but what will that matter? you will be loved, and loved truly. If Athanase seemed to you an idiot, my dear, it is that he has too many ideas; extremes meet. He lives the life of a girl of fifteen; he has never wallowed in the impurities of Paris, not he! Well, change the terms, as my poor husband used to say; it is the same thing with du Bousquier in connection with Suzanne. *You* would be calumniated; but in the case of du Bousquier, the charge would be true. Don't you understand me?"

"No more than if you were talking Greek," replied Mademoiselle Cormon, who opened her eyes wide, and strained all the forces of her intellect.

"Well, cousin, if I must dot all the i's, it is impossible for Suzanne to love du Bousquier. And if the heart counts for nothing in this affair -"

"But, cousin, what do people love with if not

Honore de Balzac

their hearts?"

Here Madame Granson said to herself, as the chevalier had previously thought: "My poor cousin is altogether too innocent; such stupidity passes all bounds! - Dear child," she continued aloud, "it seems to me that children are not conceived by the spirit only."

"Why, yes, my dear; the Holy Virgin herself -"

"But, my love, du Bousquier isn't the Holy Ghost!"

"True," said the old maid; "he is a man! - a man whose personal appearance makes him dangerous enough for his friends to advise him to marry."

"You could yourself bring about that result, cousin."

"How so?" said the old maid, with the meekness of Christian charity.

"By not receiving him in your house until he marries. You owe it to good morals and to religion to manifest under such circumstances an exemplary displeasure."

"On my return from Prebaudet we will talk further of this, my dear Madame Granson. I will consult my uncle and the Abbe Couturier," said Mademoiselle Cormon, returning to the salon, where the animation was now at its height.

The lights, the group of women in their best clothes, the solemn tone, the dignified air of the assembly, made Mademoiselle Cormon not a little proud of her company. To many persons nothing better could be seen in Paris in the highest society.

At this moment du Bousquier, who was playing whist with the chevalier and two old ladies, - Madame du Coudrai and Madame du Ronceret, - was the object of deep but silent curiosity. A few young women arrived, who, under pretext of watching the game, gazed fixedly at him in so singular a manner, though slyly, that the old bachelor began to think that there must be some deficiency in his toilet.

"Can my false front be crooked?" he asked himself, seized by one of those anxieties which beset old bachelors.

He took advantage of a lost trick, which ended a seventh rubber, to rise and leave the table.

"I can't touch a card without losing," he said. "I am decidedly too unlucky."

"But you are lucky in other ways," said the chevalier, giving him a sly look.

That speech naturally made the rounds of the salon, where every one exclaimed on the exquisite taste of the chevalier, the Prince de Talleyrand of the province.

"There's no one like Monsieur de Valois for such wit."

Du Bousquier went to look at himself in a little oblong mirror, placed above the "Deserter," but he saw nothing strange in his appearance.

After innumerable repetitions of the same text, varied in all keys, the departure of the company took place about ten o'clock, through the long antechamber, Mademoiselle Cormon conducting certain of her favorite guests to the portico. There the groups parted; some followed the Bretagne road towards the chateau; the others went in the direction of the river Sarthe. Then began the usual conversation, which for twenty years had echoed at that hour through this particular street of Alencon. It was invariably: -

"Mademoiselle Cormon looked very well to-night."

"Mademoiselle Cormon? why, I thought her rather strange."

"How that poor abbe fails! Did you notice that he slept? He does not know what cards he holds; he is getting very absent-minded."

"We shall soon have the grief of losing him."

"What a fine night! It will be a fine day to-morrow."

"Good weather for the apple-blossoms."

"You beat us; but when you play with Monsieur de Valois you never do otherwise."

"How much did he win?"

"Well, to-night, three or four francs; he never loses."

"True; and don't you know there are three hundred and sixty-five days a year? At that price his gains are the value of a farm."

"Ah! what hands we had to-night!"

"Here you are at home, monsieur and madame, how

lucky you are, while we have half the town to cross!"

"I don't pity you; you could afford a carriage, and dispense with the fatigue of going on foot."

"Ah, monsieur! we have a daughter to marry, which takes off one wheel, and the support of our son in Paris carries off another."

"You persist in making a magistrate of him?"

"What else can be done with a young man? Besides, there's no shame in serving the king."

Sometimes a discussion on ciders and flax, always couched in the same terms, and returning at the same time of year, was continued on the homeward way. If any observer of human customs had lived in this street, he would have known the months and seasons by simply overhearing the conversations.

On this occasion it was exclusively jocose; for du Bousquier, who chanced to march alone in front of the groups, was humming the well-known air, - little thinking of its appropriateness, - "Tender woman! hear the warble of the birds," etc. To some, du Bousquier was a strong man and a misjudged man. Ever since he had been confirmed in his present office by a royal decree, Monsieur du Ronceret had been in favor of du Bousquier. To others the purveyor seemed dangerous, - a man of bad habits, capable of anything. In the provinces, as in Paris, men before the public eye are like that statue in the fine allegorical tale of Addison, for which two knights on arriving near it fought; for one saw it white, the other saw it black. Then, when they were both off their horses, they saw it was white one side and black the other. A third knight coming along declared it red.

When the chevalier went home that night, he made many reflections, as follows: -

"It is high time now to spread a rumor of my marriage with Mademoiselle Cormon. It will leak out from the d'Esgrignon salon, and go straight to the bishop at Seez, and so get round through the grand vicars to the curate of Saint-Leonard's, who will be certain to tell it to the Abbe Couturier; and Mademoiselle Cormon will get the shot in her upper works. The old Marquis d'Esgrignon shall invite the Abbe de Sponde to dinner, so as to stop all gossip about Mademoiselle Cormon if I decide against her, or about me if she refuses me. The abbe shall be well cajoled; and Mademoiselle Cormon will certainly not hold out against a visit from Mademoiselle Armande, who will show her the grandeur and future chances of such an alliance. The abbe's property is undoubtedly as much as three hundred thousand; her own savings must amount to more than two hundred thousand; she has her house and Prebaudet and fifteen thousand francs a year. A word to my friend the Comte de Fontaine, and I should be mayor of Alencon to-morrow, and deputy. Then, once seated on the Right benches, we shall reach the peerage, shouting, 'Cloture!' 'Ordre!'"

As soon as she reached home Madame Granson had a lively argument with her son, who could not be made to see the connection which existed between his love and his political opinions. It was the first quarrel that had ever troubled that poor household.

CHAPTER VI

FINAL DISAPPOINTMENT
AND ITS FIRST RESULT

The next day, Mademoiselle Cormon, packed into the old carriole with Josette, and looking like a pyramid on a vast sea of parcels, drove up the rue Saint-Blaise on her way to Prebaudet, where she was overtaken by an event which hurried on her marriage, - an event entirely unlooked for by either Madame Granson, du Bousquier, Monsieur de Valois, or Mademoiselle Cormon himself. Chance is the greatest of all artificers.

The day after her arrival at Prebaudet, she was innocently employed, about eight o'clock in the morning, in listening, as she breakfasted, to the various reports of her keeper and her gardener, when Jacquelin made a violent irruption into the dining-room.

"Mademoiselle," he cried, out of breath, "Monsieur l'abbe sends you an express, the son of Mere Grosmort, with a letter. The lad left Alencon before daylight, and he has just arrived; he ran like Penelope! Can't I give him a glass of wine?"

"What can have happened, Josette? Do you think my uncle can be -"

"He couldn't write if he were," said Josette, guessing her mistress's fears.

"Quick! quick!" cried Mademoiselle Cormon, as soon as she had read the first lines. "Tell Jacquelin to harness Penelope - Get ready, Josette; pack up everything in half an hour. We must go back to town -"

"Jacquelin!" called Josette, excited by the sentiment she saw on her mistress's face.

Jacquelin, informed by Josette, came in to say, -

"But, mademoiselle, Penelope is eating her oats."

"What does that signify? I must start at once."

"But, mademoiselle, it is going to rain."

"Then we shall get wet."

"The house is on fire!" muttered Josette, piqued at the silence her mistress kept as to the contents of the letter, which she read and reread.

"Finish your coffee, at any rate, mademoiselle; don't excite your blood; just see how red you are."

"Am I red, Josette?" she said, going to a mirror, from which the quicksilver was peeling, and which presented her features to her upside down.

"Good heavens!" thought Mademoiselle Cormon, "suppose I should look ugly! Come, Josette; come, my dear, dress me at once; I want to be ready before Jacquelin has harnessed Penelope. If you can't pack my things in time, I will leave them here rather than lose a single minute."

If you have thoroughly comprehended the positive monomania to which the desire of marriage had brought Mademoiselle Cormon, you will share her emotion. The worthy uncle announced in this sudden missive that Monsieur de Troisville, of the Russian army during the Emigration, grandson of one of his best friends, was desirous of retiring to Alencon, and asked his, the abbe's hospitality, on the ground of his friendship for his grandfather, the Vicomte de Troisville. The old abbe, alarmed at the responsibility, entreated his niece to return instantly and help him to receive this guest, and do the honors of the house; for the viscount's letter had been delayed, and he might descend upon his shoulders that very night.

After reading this missive could there be a question of the demands of Prebaudet? The keeper and the gardener, witnesses to Mademoiselle Cormon's excitement, stood aside and awaited her orders. But when, as she was about to leave the room, they stopped her to ask for instructions, for the first time in her life the despotic old maid, who saw to everything at Prebaudet with her own eyes, said, to their stupefaction, "Do what you like." This from a mistress who carried her administration to the point of counting her fruits, and marking them so as to order their consumption according to the number and condition of each!

"I believe I'm dreaming," thought Josette, as she saw her mistress flying down the staircase like an elephant to which God has given wings.

Presently, in spite of a driving rain, Mademoiselle

Cormon drove away from Prebaudet, leaving her factotums with the reins on their necks. Jacquelin dared not take upon himself to hasten the usual little trot of the peaceable Penelope, who, like the beautiful queen whose name she bore, had an appearance of making as many steps backward as she made forward. Impatient with the pace, mademoiselle ordered Jacquelin in a sharp voice to drive at a gallop, with the whip, if necessary, to the great astonishment of the poor beast, so afraid was she of not having time to arrange the house suitably to receive Monsieur de Troisville. She calculated that the grandson of her uncle's friend was probably about forty years of age; a soldier just from service was undoubtedly a bachelor; and she resolved, her uncle aiding, not to let Monsieur de Troisville quit their house in the condition he entered it. Though Penelope galloped, Mademoiselle Cormon, absorbed in thoughts of her trousseau and the wedding-day, declared again and again that Jacquelin made no way at all. She twisted about in the carriole without replying to Josette's questions, and talked to herself like a person who is mentally revolving important designs.

The carriole at last arrived in the main street of Alencon, called the rue Saint-Blaise at the end toward Montagne, but near the hotel du More it takes the name of the rue de la Porte-de-Seez, and becomes the rue du Bercail as it enters the road to Brittany. If the departure of Mademoiselle Cormon made a great noise in Alencon, it is easy to imagine the uproar caused by her sudden return on the following day, in a pouring rain which beat her face without her apparently minding it. Penelope at a full gallop was observed by every one, and Jacquelin's grin, the early hour, the parcels stuffed into the carriole topsy-turvy, and the evident impatience of Mademoiselle Cormon were all noted.

The property of the house of Troisville lay between Alencon and Mortagne. Josette knew the various branches of the family. A word dropped by mademoiselle as they entered Alencon had put Josette on the scent of the affair; and a discussion having started between them, it was settled that the expected de Troisville must be between forty and forty-two years of age, a bachelor, and neither rich nor poor. Mademoiselle Cormon beheld herself speedily Vicomtesse de Troisville.

"And to think that my uncle told me nothing! thinks of nothing! inquires nothing! That's my uncle all over. He'd forget his own nose if it wasn't fastened to his face."

Have you never remarked that, under circumstances such as these, old maids become, like Richard III., keen-witted, fierce, bold, promissory, - if one may so use the word, - and, like inebriate clerks, no longer in awe of anything?

Immediately the town of Alencon, speedily informed from the farther end of the rue de Saint-Blaise to the gate of Seez of this precipitate return, accompanied by singular circumstances, was perturbed throughout its viscera, both public and domestic. Cooks, shopkeepers, street passengers, told the news from door to door; thence it rose to the upper regions. Soon the words: "Mademoiselle Cormon has returned!" burst like a bombshell into all households. At that moment Jacquelin was descending from his wooden seat (polished by a process unknown to cabinet-makers), on which he perched in front of the carriole. He opened the great green gate, round at the top, and closed in sign of mourning; for during Mademoiselle Cormon's absence the evening assemblies did not take place. The faithful invited the Abbe de Sponde to their several houses; and Monsieur de Valois paid his debt by inviting him to dine at the Marquis d'Esgrignon's. Jacquelin, having opened the gate, called familiarly to Penelope, whom he had left in the middle of the street. That animal, accustomed to this proceeding, turned in of herself, and circled round the courtyard in a manner to avoid injuring the flower-bed. Jacquelin then took her bridle, and led the carriage to the portico.

"Mariette!" cried Mademoiselle Cormon.

"Mademoiselle!" exclaimed Mariette, who was occupied in closing the gate.

"Has the gentleman arrived?"

"No, mademoiselle."

"Where's my uncle?"

"He is at church, mademoiselle."

Jacquelin and Josette were by this time on the first step of the portico, holding out their hands to manoeuvre the exit of their mistress from the carriole as she pulled herself up by the sides of the vehicle and clung to the curtains. Mademoiselle then threw herself into their arms; because for the last two years she dared not risk her weight on the iron step, affixed to the frame of the carriage by a horrible mechanism of clumsy bolts.

When Mademoiselle Cormon reached the level of the

portico she looked about her courtyard with an air of satisfaction.

"Come, come, Mariette, leave that gate alone; I want you."

"There's something in the wind," whispered Jacquelin, as Mariette passed the carriole.

"Mariette, what provisions have you in the house?" asked Mademoiselle Cormon, sitting down on the bench in the long antechamber like a person overcome with fatigue.

"I haven't anything," replied Mariette, with her hands on her hips. "Mademoiselle knows very well that during her absence Monsieur l'abbe dines out every day. Yesterday I went to fetch him from Mademoiselle Armande's."

"Where is he now?"

"Monsieur l'abbe? Why, at church; he won't be in before three o'clock."

"He thinks of nothing! he ought to have told you to go to market. Mariette, go at once; and without wasting money, don't spare it; get all there is that is good and delicate. Go to the diligence office and see if you can send for pates; and I want shrimps from the Brillante. What o'clock is it?"

"A quarter to nine."

"Good heavens! Mariette, don't stop to chatter. The person my uncle expects may arrive at any moment. If we had to give him breakfast, where should we be with nothing in the house?"

Mariette turned back to Penelope in a lather, and looked at Jacquelin as if she would say, "Mademoiselle has put her hand on a husband *this* time."

"Now, Josette," continued the old maid, "let us see where we had better put Monsieur de Troisville to sleep."

With what joy she said the words, "Put Monsieur de Troisville" (pronounced Treville) "to sleep." How many ideas in those few words! The old maid was bathed in hope.

"Will you put him in the green chamber?"

"The bishop's room? No; that's too near mine," said Mademoiselle Cormon. "All very well for monseigneur; he's a saintly man."

"Give him your uncle's room."

"Oh, that's so bare; it is actually indecent."

"Well, then, mademoiselle, why not arrange a bed in your boudoir? It is easily done; and there's a fire-place. Moreau can certainly find in his warerooms a bed to match the hangings."

"You are right, Josette. Go yourself to Moreau; consult with him what to do; I authorize you to get what is wanted. If the bed could be put up to-night without Monsieur de Troisville observing it (in case Monsieur de Troisville arrives while Moreau is here), I should like it. If Moreau won't engage to do this, then I must put Monsieur de Troisville in the green room, although Monsieur de Troisville would be so very near to me."

Josette was departing when her mistress recalled her.

"Stop! explain the matter to Jacquelin," she cried, in a loud nervous tone. "Tell *him* to go to Moreau; I must be dressed! Fancy if Monsieur de Troisville surprised me as I am now! and my uncle not here to receive him! Oh, uncle, uncle! Come, Josette; come and dress me at once."

"But Penelope?" said Josette, imprudently.

"Always Penelope! Penelope this, Penelope that! Is Penelope the mistress of this house?"

"But she is all of a lather, and she hasn't had time to eat her oats."

"Then let her starve!" cried Mademoiselle Cormon; "provided I marry," she thought to herself.

Hearing these words, which seemed to her like homicide, Josette stood still for a moment, speechless. Then, at a gesture from her mistress, she ran headlong down the steps of the portico.

"The devil is in her, Jacquelin," were the first words she uttered.

Thus all things conspired on this fateful day to produce the great scenic effect which decided the future life of Mademoiselle Cormon. The town was already topsy-turvy in mind, as a consequence of the five extraordinary circumstances which accompanied Mademoiselle Cormon's return; to wit, the pouring rain; Penelope at a gallop, in a lather, and blown; the early hour; the parcels half-packed; and the singular air of the excited old maid. But when Mariette made an invasion of the market, and bought all the best things; when Jacquelin went to the principal upholsterer in Alencon, two doors from the church, in search of a bed, - there was matter for the gravest conjectures. These extraordinary events were discussed on all sides; they occupied the minds of every one, even Mademoiselle Armande herself, with whom was Monsieur de Valois. Within two days the town of Alencon had been agitated by such startling events that certain good women were heard to remark that the world was coming to an end. This last news, however, resolved itself into a single question, "What is happening at the Cormons?"

The Abbe de Sponde, adroitly questioned when he left Saint-Leonard's to take his daily walk with the Abbe Couturier, replied with his usual kindliness that he expected the Vicomte de Troisville, a nobleman in the service of Russia during the Emigration, who was returning to Alencon to settle there. From two to five o'clock a species of labial telegraphy went on throughout the town; and all the inhabitants learned that Mademoiselle Cormon had at last found a husband by letter, and was about to marry the Vicomte de Troisville. Some said, "Moreau has sold them a bed." The bed was six feet wide in that quarter; it was four feet wide at Madame Granson's, in the rue du Bercail; but it was reduced to a simple couch at Monsieur du Ronceret's, where du Bousquier was dining. The lesser bourgeoisie declared that the cost was eleven hundred francs. But generally it was thought that, as to this, rumor was counting the chickens before they were hatched. In other quarters it was said that Mariette had made such a raid on the market that the price of carp had risen. At the end of the rue Saint-Blaise, Penelope had dropped dead. This decease was doubted in the house of the receiver-general; but at the Prefecture it was authenticated that the poor beast had expired as she turned into the courtyard of the hotel Cormon, with such velocity had the old maid flown to meet her husband. The harness-maker, who lived at the corner of the rue de Seez, was bold enough to call at the house and ask if anything had happened to Mademoiselle Cormon's carriage, in order to discover whether Penelope was really dead. From the end of the rue Saint-Blaise to the end of the rue du Bercail, it was then made known that, thanks to Jacquelin's devotion, Penelope, that silent victim of her mistress's impetuosity, still lived, though she seemed to be suffering.

Along the road to Brittany the Vicomte de Troisville was stated to be a younger son without a penny, for the estates in Perche belonged to the Marquis de Troisville, peer of France, who had children; the marriage would be, therefore, an enormous piece of luck for a poor emigre. The aristocracy along that road approved of the marriage; Mademoiselle Cormon could not do better with her money. But among the Bourgeoisie, the Vicomte de Troisville was a Russian general who had fought against France, and was now returning with a great fortune made at the court of Saint-Petersburg; he was a *foreigner*; one of those *allies* so hated by the liberals; the Abbe de Sponde had slyly negotiated this marriage. All the persons who had a right to call upon Mademoiselle Cormon determined to do so that very evening.

During this transurban excitement, which made that of Suzanne almost a forgotten affair, Mademoiselle was not less agitated; she was filled with a variety of novel emotions. Looking about her salon, dining-room, and boudoir, cruel apprehensions took possession of her. A species of demon showed her with a sneer her old-fashioned luxury. The handsome things she had admired from her youth up she suddenly suspected of age and absurdity. In short, she felt that fear which takes possession of nearly all authors when they read over a work they have hitherto thought proof against every exacting or blase critic: new situations seem timeworn; the best-turned and most highly polished phrases limp and squint; metaphors and images grin or contradict each other; whatsoever is false strikes the eye. In like manner this poor woman trembled lest she should see on the lips of Monsieur de Troisville a smile of contempt for this episcopal salon; she dreaded the cold look he might cast over that ancient dining-room; in short, she feared the frame might injure and age the portrait. Suppose these antiquities should cast a reflected light of old age upon herself? This question made her flesh creep. She would gladly, at that moment, spend half her savings on refitting her house if some fairy wand could do it in a moment. Where is the general who has not trembled on the eve of a battle? The poor woman was now between her Austerlitz and her Waterloo.

"Madame la Vicomtesse de Troisville," she said to herself; "a noble name! Our property will go to a good family, at any rate."

She fell a prey to an irritation which made every fibre of her nerves quiver to all their papillae, long sunk in flesh. Her blood, lashed by this new hope, was in motion. She felt the strength to converse, if necessary, with Monsieur de Troisville.

It is useless to relate the activity with which Josette, Jacquelin, Mariette, Moreau, and his agents went about their functions. It was like the busyness of ants about their eggs. All that daily care had already rendered neat and clean was again gone over and brushed and rubbed and scrubbed. The china of ceremony saw the light; the damask linen marked "A, B, C" was drawn from depths where it lay under a triple guard of wrappings, still further defended by formidable lines of pins. Above all, Mademoiselle Cormon sacrificed on the altar of her hopes three bottles of the famous liqueurs of Madame Amphoux, the most illustrious of all the distillers of the tropics, - a name very dear to gourmets. Thanks to the devotion of her lieutenants, mademoiselle was soon ready for the conflict. The different weapons - furniture, cookery, provisions, in short, all the various munitions of war, together with a body of reserve forces - were ready along the whole line. Jacquelin, Mariette, and Josette received orders to appear in full dress. The garden was raked. The old maid regretted that she couldn't come to an understanding with the nightingales nesting in the trees, in order to obtain their finest trilling.

At last, about four o'clock, at the very moment when the Abbe de Sponde returned home, and just as mademoiselle began to think she had set the table with the best plate and linen and prepared the choicest dishes to no purpose, the click-clack of a postilion was heard in the Val-Noble.

"'Tis he!" she said to herself, the snap of the whip echoing in her heart.

True enough; heralded by all this gossip, a post-chaise, in which was a single gentleman, made so great a sensation coming down the rue Saint-Blaise and turning into the rue du Cours that several little gamains and some grown persons followed it, and stood in groups about the gate of the hotel Cormon to see it enter. Jacquelin, who foresaw his own marriage in that of his mistress, had also heard the click-clack in the rue Saint-Blaise, and had opened wide the gates into the courtyard. The postilion, a friend of his, took pride in making a fine turn-in, and drew up sharply before the portico. The abbe came forward to greet his guest, whose carriage was emptied with a speed that high-waymen might put into the operation; the chaise itself was rolled into the coach-house, the gates closed, and in a few moments all signs of Monsieur de Troisville's arrival had disappeared. Never did two chemicals blend into each other with greater rapidity than the hotel Cormon displayed in absorbing the Vicomte de Troisville.

Mademoiselle, whose heart was beating like a lizard caught by a herdsman, sat heroically still on her sofa, beside the fire in the salon. Josette opened the door; and the Vicomte de Troisville, followed by the Abbe de Sponde, presented himself to the eyes of the spinster.

"Niece, this is Monsieur le Vicomte de Troisville, the grandson of one of my old schoolmates; Monsieur de Troisville, my niece, Mademoiselle Cormon."

"Ah! that good uncle; how well he does it!" thought Rose-Marie-Victoire.

The Vicomte de Troisville was, to paint him in two

words, du Bousquier ennobled. Between the two men there was precisely the difference which separates the vulgar style from the noble style. If they had both been present, the most fanatic liberal would not have denied the existence of aristocracy. The viscount's strength had all the distinction of elegance; his figure had preserved its magnificent dignity. He had blue eyes, black hair, an olive skin, and looked to be about forty-six years of age. You might have thought him a handsome Spaniard preserved in the ice of Russia. His manner, carriage, and attitude, all denoted a diplomat who had seen Europe. His dress was that of a well-bred traveller. As he seemed fatigued, the abbe offered to show him to his room, and was much amazed when his niece threw open the door of the boudoir, transformed into a bedroom.

Mademoiselle Cormon and her uncle then left the noble stranger to attend to his own affairs, aided by Jacquelin, who brought up his luggage, and went themselves to walk beside the river until their guest had made his toilet. Although the Abbe de Sponde chanced to be even more absent-minded than usual, Mademoiselle Cormon was not less preoccupied. They both walked on in silence. The old maid had never before met any man as seductive as this Olympean viscount. She might have said to herself, as the Germans do, "This is my ideal!" instead of which she felt herself bound from head to foot, and could only say, "Here's my affair!" Then she flew to Mariette to know if the dinner could be put back a while without loss of excellence.

"Uncle, your Monsieur de Troisville is very amiable," she said, on returning.

"Why, niece, he hasn't as yet said a word."

"But you can see it in his ways, his manners, his face. Is he a bachelor?"

"I'm sure I don't know," replied the abbe, who was thinking of a discussion on mercy, lately begun between the Abbe Couturier and himself. "Monsieur de Troisville wrote me that he wanted to buy a house here. If he was married, he wouldn't come alone on such an errand," added the abbe, carelessly, not conceiving the idea that his niece could be thinking of marriage.

"Is he rich?"

"He is a younger son of the younger branch," replied her uncle. "His grandfather commanded a squadron, but the father of this young man made a bad marriage."

"Young man!" exclaimed the old maid. "It seems to me, uncle, that he must be at least forty-five." She felt the strongest desire to put their years on a par.

"Yes," said the abbe; "but to a poor priest of seventy, Rose, a man of forty seems a youth."

All Alencon knew by this time that Monsieur de Troisville had arrived at the Cormons. The traveller soon rejoined his hosts, and began to admire the Brillante, the garden, and the house.

"Monsieur l'abbe," he said, "my whole ambition is to have a house like this." The old maid fancied a declaration lurked in that speech, and she lowered her eyes. "You must enjoy it very much, mademoiselle," added the viscount.

"How could it be otherwise? It has been in our family since 1574, the period at which one of our ancestors, steward to the Duc d'Alencon, acquired the land and built the house," replied Mademoiselle Cormon. "It is built on piles," she added.

Jacquelin announced dinner. Monsieur de Troisville offered his arm to the happy woman, who endeavored not to lean too heavily upon it; she feared, as usual, to seem to make advances.

"Everything is so harmonious here," said the viscount, as he seated himself at table.

"Yes, our trees are full of birds, which give us concerts for nothing; no one ever frightens them; and the nightingales sing at night," said Mademoiselle Cormon.

"I was speaking of the interior of the house," remarked the viscount, who did not trouble himself to observe Mademoiselle Cormon, and therefore did not perceive the dulness of her mind. "Everything is so in keeping, - the tones of color, the furniture, the general character."

"But it costs a great deal; taxes are enormous," responded the excellent woman.

"Ah! taxes are high, are they?" said the viscount, preoccupied with his own ideas.

"I don't know," replied the abbe. "My niece manages the property of each of us."

Honore de Balzac

"Taxes are not of much importance to the rich," said Mademoiselle Cormon, not wishing to be thought miserly. "As for the furniture, I shall leave it as it is, and change nothing, - unless I marry; and then, of course, everything here must suit the husband."

"You have noble principles, mademoiselle," said the viscount, smiling. "You will make one happy man."

"No one ever made to me such a pretty speech," thought the old maid.

The viscount complimented Mademoiselle Cormon on the excellence of her service and the admirable arrangements of the house, remarking that he had supposed the provinces behind the age in that respect; but, on the contrary, he found them, as the English say, "very comfortable."

"What can that word mean?" she thought. "Oh, where is the chevalier to explain it to me? 'Comfortable,' - there seem to be several words in it. Well, courage!" she said to herself. "I can't be expected to answer a foreign language - But," she continued aloud, feeling her tongue untied by the eloquence which nearly all human creatures find in momentous circumstances, "we have a very brilliant society here, monsieur. It assembles at my house, and you shall judge of it this evening, for some of my faithful friends have no doubt heard of my return and your arrival. Among them is the Chevalier de Valois, a seigneur of the old court, a man of infinite wit and taste; then there is Monsieur le Marquis d'Esgrignon and Mademoiselle Armande, his sister" (she bit her tongue with vexation), - "a woman remarkable in her way," she added. "She resolved to remain unmarried in order to leave all her fortune to her brother and nephew."

"Ah!" exclaimed the viscount. "Yes, the d'Esgrignons, - I remember them."

"Alencon is very gay," continued the old maid, now fairly launched. "There's much amusement: the receiver-general gives balls; the prefect is an amiable man; and Monseigneur the bishop sometimes honors us with a visit -"

"Well, then," said the viscount, smiling, "I have done wisely to come back, like the hare, to die in my form."

"Yes," she said. "I, too, attach myself or I die."

The viscount smiled.

"Ah!" thought the old maid, "all is well; he understands me."

The conversation continued on generalities. By one of those mysterious unknown and undefinable faculties, Mademoiselle Cormon found in her brain, under the pressure of her desire to be agreeable, all the phrases and opinions of the Chevalier de Valois. It was like a duel in which the devil himself pointed the pistol. Never was any adversary better aimed at. The viscount was far too well-bred to speak of the excellence of the dinner; but his silence was praise. As he drank the delicious wines which Jacquelin served to him profusely, he seemed to feel he was with friends, and to meet them with pleasure; for the true connoisseur does not applaud, he enjoys. He inquired the price of land, of houses, of estates; he made Mademoiselle Cormon describe at length the confluence of the Sarthe and the Brillante; he expressed surprise that the town was placed so far from the river, and seemed to be much interested in the topography of the place.

The silent abbe left his niece to throw the dice of conversation; and she truly felt that she pleased Monsieur de Troisville, who smiled at her gracefully, and committed himself during this dinner far more than her most eager suitors had ever done in ten days. Imagine, therefore, the little attentions with which he was petted; you might have thought him a cherished lover, whose return brought joy to the household. Mademoiselle foresaw the moment when the viscount wanted bread; she watched his every look; when he turned his head she adroitly put upon his plate a portion of some dish he seemed to like; had he been a gourmand, she would almost have killed him; but what a delightful specimen of the attentions she would show to a husband! She did not commit the folly of depreciating herself; on the contrary, she set every sail bravely, ran up all her flags, assumed the bearing of the queen of Alencon, and boasted of her excellent preserves. In fact, she fished for compliments in speaking of herself, for she saw that she pleased the viscount; the truth being that her eager desire had so transformed her that she became almost a woman.

At dessert she heard, not without emotions of delight, certain sounds in the antechamber and salon which denoted the arrival of her usual guests. She called the attention of her uncle and Monsieur de Troisville to this prompt attendance as a proof of the affection that was felt for her; whereas it was really the result of the poignant curiosity which had seized upon the town. Impatient to show herself in all her glory, Mademoiselle Cormon told Jacquelin to serve coffee and liqueurs in the salon, where he presently set out, in view of the whole company, a magnificent liqueur-stand of Dresden china which saw the light only twice a year. This circumstance was taken note of by the company, standing ready to gossip over the merest trifle: -

"The deuce!" muttered du Bousquier. "Actually Madame Amphoux's liqueurs, which they only serve at the four church festivals!"

"Undoubtedly the marriage was arranged a year ago by letter," said the chief-justice du Ronceret. "The post-master tells me his office has received letters postmarked Odessa for more than a year."

Madame Granson trembled. The Chevalier de Valois, though he had dined with the appetite of four men, turned pale even to the left section of his face. Feeling that he was about to betray himself, he said hastily, -

"Don't you think it is very cold to-day? I am almost frozen."

"The neighborhood of Russia, perhaps," said du Bousquier.

The chevalier looked at him as if to say, "Well played!"

Mademoiselle Cormon appeared so radiant, so triumphant, that the company thought her handsome. This extraordinary brilliancy was not the effect of sentiment only. Since early morning her blood had been whirling tempestuously within her, and her nerves were agitated by the presentiment of some great crisis. It required all these circumstances combined to make her so unlike herself. With what joy did she now make her solemn presentation of the viscount to the chevalier, the chevalier to the viscount, and all Alencon to Monsieur de Troisville, and Monsieur de Troisville to all Alencon!

By an accident wholly explainable, the viscount and chevalier, aristocrats by nature, came instantly into unison; they recognized each other at once as men belonging to the same sphere. Accordingly, they began to converse together, standing before the fireplace. A circle formed around them; and their conversation, though uttered in a low voice, was listened to in religious silence. To give the effect of this scene it is necessary to dramatize it, and to picture Mademoiselle Cormon occupied in pouring out the coffee of her imaginary suitor, with her back to the fireplace.

Monsieur de Valois. "Monsieur le vicomte has come, I am told, to settle in Alencon?"

Monsieur de Troisville. "Yes, monsieur, I am looking for a house." [Mademoiselle Cormon, cup in hand, turns round.] "It must be a large house" [Mademoiselle Cormon offers him the cup] "to lodge my whole family." [The eyes of the old maid are troubled.]

Monsieur de Valois. "Are you married?"

Monsieur de Troisville. "Yes, for the last sixteen years, to a daughter of the Princess Scherbellof."

Mademoiselle Cormon fainted; du Bousquier, who saw her stagger, sprang forward and received her in his arms; some one opened the door and allowed him to pass out with his enormous burden. The fiery republican, instructed by Josette, found strength to carry the old maid to her bedroom, where he laid her out on the bed. Josette, armed with scissors, cut the corset, which was terribly tight. Du Bousquier flung water on Mademoiselle Cormon's face and bosom, which, released from the corset, overflowed like the Loire in flood. The poor woman opened her eyes, saw du Bousquier, and gave a cry of modesty at the sight of him. Du Bousquier retired at once, leaving six women, at the head of whom was Madame Granson, radiant with joy, to take care of the invalid.

What had the Chevalier de Valois been about all this time? Faithful to his system, he had covered the retreat.

"That poor Mademoiselle Cormon," he said to Monsieur de Troisville, gazing at the assembly, whose laughter was repressed by his cool aristocratic glances, "her blood is horribly out of order; she wouldn't be bled before going to Prebaudet (her estate), - and see the result!"

"She came back this morning in the rain," said the Abbe de Sponde, "and she may have taken cold. It won't be anything; it is only a little upset she is subject to."

"She told me yesterday she had not had one for three months, adding that she was afraid it would play her a trick at last," said the chevalier.

"Ha! so you are married?" said Jacquelin to himself as he looked at Monsieur de Troisville, who was quietly sipping his coffee.

The faithful servant espoused his mistress's disappointment; he divined it, and he promptly carried away the liqueurs of Madame Amphoux, which were offered to a bachelor, and not to the husband of a Russian woman.

All these details were noticed and laughed at. The Abbe de Sponde knew the object of Monsieur de Troisville's journey; but, absent-minded as usual, he forgot it, not supposing that his niece could have the slightest interest in Monsieur de Troisville's marriage. As for the viscount, preoccupied with the object of his journey, and, like many husbands, not eager to talk about his wife, he had had no occasion to say he was married; besides, he would naturally suppose that Mademoiselle Cormon knew it.

Du Bousquier reappeared, and was questioned furiously. One of the six women came down soon after, and announced that Mademoiselle Cormon was much better, and that the doctor had come. She intended to stay in bed, as it was necessary to bleed her. The salon was now full. Mademoiselle Cormon's absence allowed the ladies present to discuss the tragi-comic scene - embellished, extended, historified, embroidered, wreathed, colored, and adorned - which had just taken place, and which, on the morrow, was destined to occupy all Alencon.

"That good Monsieur du Bousquier! how well he carried you!" said Josette to her mistress. "He was really pale at the sight of you; he loves you still."

That speech served as closure to this solemn and terrible evening.

Throughout the morning of the next day every circumstance of the late comedy was known in the household of Alencon, and - let us say it to the shame of that town, - they caused inextinguishable laughter. But on that day Mademoiselle Cormon (much benefited by the bleeding) would have seemed sublime even to the boldest scoffers, had they witnessed the noble dignity, the splendid Christian resignation which influenced her as she gave her arm to her involuntary deceiver to go into breakfast. Cruel jesters! why could you not have seen her as she said to the viscount, -

"Madame de Troisville will have difficulty in finding a suitable house; do me the favor, monsieur, of accepting the use of mine during the time you are in search of yours."

"But, mademoiselle, I have two sons and two daughters; we should greatly inconvenience you."

"Pray do not refuse me," she said earnestly.

"I made you the same offer in the answer I wrote to your letter," said the abbe; "but you did not receive it."

"What, uncle! then you knew -"

The poor woman stopped. Josette sighed. Neither the viscount nor the abbe observed anything amiss. After breakfast the Abbe de Sponde carried off his guest, as agreed upon the previous evening, to show him the various houses in Alencon which could be bought, and the lots of lands on which he might build.

Left alone in the salon, Mademoiselle Cormon said to Josette, with a deeply distressed air, "My child, I am now the talk of the whole town."

"Well, then, mademoiselle, you should marry."

"But I am not prepared to make a choice."

"Bah! if I were in your place, I should take Monsieur du Bousquier."

"Josette, Monsieur de Valois says he is so republican."

"They don't know what they say, your gentlemen: sometimes they declare that he robbed the republic; he couldn't love it if he did that," said Josette, departing.

"That girl has an amazing amount of sense," thought Mademoiselle Cormon, who remained alone, a prey to her perplexities.

She saw plainly that a prompt marriage was the only way to silence the town. This last checkmate, so evidently mortifying, was of a nature to drive her into some extreme action; for persons deficient in mind find difficulty in getting out of any path, either good or evil, into which they have entered.

Each of the two old bachelors had fully understood the situation in which Mademoiselle Cormon was about to find herself; consequently, each resolved to call in the course of that morning to ask after her health, and take occasion, in bachelor language, to "press his point." Monsieur de Valois considered that such an occasion demanded a painstaking toilet; he therefore took a bath and groomed himself with extraordinary care. For the first and last time Cesarine observed him putting on with incredible art a suspicion of rouge. Du Bousquier, on the other hand, that coarse republican, spurred by a brisk will, paid no attention to his dress, and arrived the first.

Such little things decide the fortunes of men, as they do of empires. Kellerman's charge at Marengo, Blucher's arrival at Waterloo, Louis XIV.'s disdain for Prince Eugene, the rector of Denain, - all these great causes of fortune or catastrophe history has recorded; but no one ever profits by them to avoid the small neglects of their own life. Consequently, observe what happens: the Duchesse de Langeais (see "History of the Thirteen") makes herself a nun for the lack of ten minutes' patience; Judge Popinot (see "Commission in Lunacy") puts off till the morrow the duty of examining the Marquis d'Espard; Charles Grandet (see "Eugenie Grandet") goes to Paris from Bordeaux instead of returning by Nantes; and such events are called chance or fatality! A touch of rouge carefully applied destroyed the hopes of the Chevalier de Valois; could that nobleman perish in any other way? He had lived by the Graces, and he was doomed to die by their hand. While the chevalier was giving this last touch to his toilet the rough du Bousquier was entering the salon of the desolate old maid. This entrance produced a thought in Mademoiselle Cormon's mind which was favorable to the republican, although in all other respects the Chevalier de Valois held the advantages.

"God wills it!" she said piously, on seeing du Bousquier.

"Mademoiselle, you will not, I trust, think my eagerness importunate. I could not trust to my stupid Rene to bring news of your condition, and therefore I have come myself."

"I am perfectly recovered," she replied, in a tone of emotion. "I thank you, Monsieur du Bousquier," she added, after a slight pause, and in a significant tone of voice, "for the trouble you have taken, and for that which I gave you yesterday -"

She remembered having been in his arms, and that again seemed to her an order from heaven. She had been seen for the first time by a man with her laces cut, her treasures violently bursting from their casket.

"I carried you with such joy that you seemed to me light."

Here Mademoiselle Cormon looked at du Bousquier as she had never yet looked at any man in the world. Thus encouraged, the purveyor cast upon the old maid a glance which reached her heart.

"I would," he said, "that that moment had given me the right to keep you as mine forever" [she listened with a delighted air]; "as you lay fainting upon that bed, you were enchanting. I have never in my life seen a more beautiful person, - and I have seen many handsome women. Plump ladies have this advantage: they are superb to look upon; they have only to show themselves and they triumph."

"I fear you are making fun of me," said the old maid, "and that is not kind when all the town will probably misinterpret what happened to me yesterday."

"As true as my name is du Bousquier, mademoiselle, I have never changed in my feelings toward you; and your first refusal has not discouraged me."

The old maid's eyes were lowered. There was a moment of cruel silence for du Bousquier, and then Mademoiselle Cormon decided on her course. She raised her eyelids; tears flowed from her eyes, and she gave du Bousquier a tender glance.

"If that is so, monsieur," she said, in a trembling voice, "promise me to live in a Christian manner, and not oppose my religious customs, but to leave me the right to select my confessors, and I will grant you my hand"; as she said the words, she held it out to him.

Du Bousquier seized the good fat hand so full of money, and kissed it solemnly.

"But," she said, allowing him to kiss it, "one thing more I must require of you."

"If it is a possible thing, it is granted," replied the purveyor.

"Alas!" returned the old maid. "For my sake, I must ask you to take upon yourself a sin which I feel to be enormous, - for to lie is one of the capital sins. But you will confess it, will you not? We will do penance for it together" [they looked at each other tenderly]. "Besides, it may be one of those lies which the Church permits as necessary -"

"Can she be as Suzanne says she is?" thought du Bousquier. "What luck! Well, mademoiselle, what is it?" he said aloud.

"That you will take upon yourself to -"

"What?"

"To say that this marriage has been agreed upon between us for the last six months."

"Charming woman," said the purveyor, in the tone of a man willing to devote himself, "such sacrifices can be made only for a creature adored these ten years."

"In spite of my harshness?" she said.

"Yes, in spite of your harshness."

"Monsieur du Bousquier, I have misjudged you."

Again she held out the fat red hand, which du Bousquier kissed again.

At this moment the door opened; the betrothed pair, looking round to see who entered, beheld the delightful, but tardy Chevalier de Valois.

"Ah!" he said, on entering, "I see you are about to be up, fair queen."

She smiled at the chevalier, feeling a weight upon her heart. Monsieur de Valois, remarkably young and seductive, had the air of a Lauzun re-entering the apartments of the Grande Mademoiselle in the Palais-Royal.

"Hey! dear du Bousquier," said he, in a jaunty tone, so sure was he of success, "Monsieur de Troisville and the Abbe de Sponde are examining your house like appraisers."

"Faith!" said du Bousquier, "if the Vicomte de Troisville wants it, it it is his for forty thousand francs.

It is useless to me now. If mademoiselle will permit - it must soon be known - Mademoiselle, may I tell it? - Yes! Well, then, be the first, *my dear Chevalier*, to hear" [Mademoiselle Cormon dropped her eyes] "of the honor that mademoiselle has done me, the secret of which I have kept for some months. We shall be married in a few days; the contract is already drawn, and we shall sign it to-morrow. You see, therefore, that my house in the rue du Cygne is useless to me. I have been privately looking for a purchaser for some time; and the Abbe de Sponde, who knew that fact, has naturally taken Monsieur de Troisville to see the house."

This falsehood bore such an appearance of truth that the chevalier was taken in by it. That "my dear chevalier" was like the revenge taken by Peter the Great on Charles XII. at Pultawa for all his past defeats. Du Bousquier revenged himself deliciously for the thousand little shafts he had long borne in silence; but in his triumph he made a lively youthful gesture by running his hands through his hair, and in so doing he - knocked aside his false front.

"I congratulate you both," said the chevalier, with an agreeable air; "and I wish that the marriage may end like a fairy tale: *They were happy ever after, and had - many - children!*" So saying, he took a pinch of snuff. "But, monsieur," he added satirically, "you forget - that you are wearing a false front."

Du Bousquier blushed. The false front was hanging half a dozen inches from his skull. Mademoiselle Cormon raised her eyes, saw that skull in all its nudity, and lowered them, abashed. Du Bousquier cast upon the chevalier the most venomous look that toad ever darted on its prey.

"Dogs of aristocrats who despise me," thought he, "I'll crush you some day."

The chevalier thought he had recovered his advantage. But Mademoiselle Cormon was not a woman to understand the connection which the chevalier intimated between his congratulatory wish and the false front. Besides, even if she had comprehended it, her word was passed, her hand given. Monsieur de Valois saw at once that all was lost. The innocent woman, with the two now silent men before her, wished, true to her sense of duty, to amuse them.

"Why not play a game of piquet together?" she said artlessly, without the slightest malice.

Du Bousquier smiled, and went, as the future master of the house, to fetch the piquet table. Whether the Chevalier de Valois lost his head, or whether he wanted to stay and study the causes of his disaster and remedy it, certain it is that he allowed himself to be led like a lamb to the slaughter. He had received the most violent knock-down blow that ever struck a man; any nobleman would have lost his senses for less.

The Abbe de Sponde and the Vicomte de Troisville soon returned. Mademoiselle Cormon instantly rose, hurried into the antechamber, and took her uncle apart to tell him her resolution. Learning that the house in the rue du Cygne exactly suited the viscount, she begged her future husband to do her the kindness to tell him that her uncle knew it was for sale. She dared not confide that lie to the abbe, fearing his absent-mindedness. The lie, however, prospered better than if it had been a virtuous action. In the course of that evening all Alencon heard the news. For the last four days the town had had as much to think of as during the fatal days of 1814 and 1815. Some laughed; others admitted the marriage. These blamed it; those approved it. The middle classes of Alencon rejoiced; they regarded it as a victory. The next day, among friends, the Chevalier de Valois said a cruel thing: -

"The Cormons end as they began; there's only a hand's breadth between a steward and a purveyor."

CHAPTER VII

OTHER RESULTS

The news of Mademoiselle Cormon's choice stabbed poor Athanase Granson to the heart; but he showed no outward sign of the terrible agitation within him. When he first heard of the marriage he was at the house of the chief-justice, du Ronceret, where his mother was playing boston. Madame Granson looked at her son in a mirror, and thought him pale; but he had been so all day, for a vague rumor of the matter had already reached him.

Mademoiselle Cormon was the card on which Athanase had staked his life; and the cold presentiment of a catastrophe was already upon him. When the soul and the imagination have magnified a misfortune and made it too heavy for the shoulders and the brain to bear; when a hope long cherished, the realization of which would pacify the vulture feeding on the heart, is balked, and the man has faith neither in himself, despite his powers, nor in the future, despite of the Divine power, - then that man is lost. Athanase was a fruit of the Imperial system of education. Fatality, the Emperor's religion, had filtered down from the throne to the lowest ranks of the army and the benches of the lyceums. Athanase sat still, with his eyes fixed on Madame du Ronceret's cards, in a stupor that might so well pass for indifference that Madame Granson herself was deceived about his feelings. This apparent unconcern explained her son's refusal to make a sacrifice for this marriage of his *liberal* opinions, - the term "liberal" having lately been created for the Emperor Alexander by, I think, Madame de Stael, through the lips of Benjamin Constant.

After that fatal evening the young man took to rambling among the picturesque regions of the Sarthe, the banks of which are much frequented by sketchers who come to Alencon for points of view. Windmills are there, and the river is gay in the meadows. The shores of the Sarthe are bordered with beautiful trees, well grouped. Though the landscape is flat, it is not without those modest graces which distinguish France, where the eye is never wearied by the brilliancy of Oriental skies, nor saddened by constant fog. The place is solitary. In the provinces no one pays much attention to a fine view, either because provincials are blases on the beauty around them, or because they have no poesy in their souls. If there exists in the provinces a mall, a promenade, a vantage-ground from which a fine view can be obtained, that is the point to which no one goes. Athanase was fond of this solitude, enlivened by the sparkling water, where the fields were the first to green under the earliest smiling of the springtide sun. Those persons who saw him sitting beneath a poplar, and who noticed the vacant eye which he turned to them, would say to Madame Granson: -

"Something is the matter with your son."

"I know what it is," the mother would reply; hinting that he was meditating over some great work.

Athanase no longer took part in politics: he ceased to have opinions; but he appeared at times quite gay, - gay with the satire of those who think to insult a whole world with their own individual scorn. This young man, outside of all the ideas and all the pleasures of the provinces, interested few persons; he was not even an object of curiosity. If persons spoke of him to his mother, it was for her sake, not his. There was not a single soul in Alencon that sympathized with his; not a woman, not a friend came near to dry his tears; they dropped into the Sarthe. If the gorgeous Suzanne had happened that way, how many young miseries might have been born of the meeting! for the two would surely have loved each other.

She did come, however. Suzanne's ambition was early excited by the tale of a strange adventure which had happened at the tavern of the More, - a tale which had taken possession of her childish brain. A Parisian woman, beautiful as the angels, was sent by Fouche to entangle the Marquis de Montauran, otherwise called "The Gars," in a love-affair (see "The Chouans"). She met him at the tavern of the More on his return from an expedition to Mortagne; she cajoled him, made him love her, and then betrayed him. That fantastic power - the power of beauty over mankind; in fact, the whole story of Marie de Verneuil and the Gars - dazzled Suzanne; she longed to grow up in order to play upon men. Some months after her hasty departure she passed through her native town with an artist on his way to Brittany. She wanted to see Fougeres, where the adventure of the Marquis de Montauran culminated, and to stand upon the scene of that picturesque war, the tragedies of which, still so little known, had filled her childish mind. Besides this, she had a fancy to pass through Alencon so elegantly equipped that no one could recognize her; to put her mother above the reach of necessity, and also to send to poor Athanase, in a delicate manner, a sum of money, - which in our age is to genius what in the middle ages was the charger and the coat of mail that Rebecca conveyed to Ivanhoe.

One month passed away in the strangest uncertainties respecting the marriage of Mademoiselle Cormon. A party of unbelievers denied the marriage altogether; the believers, on the other hand, affirmed it. At the end of two weeks, the faction of unbelief received a vigorous blow in the sale of du Bousquier's house to the Marquis de Troisville, who only wanted a simple establishment in Alencon, intending to go to Paris after the death of the Princess Scherbellof; he proposed to await that inheritance in retirement, and then to reconstitute his estates. This seemed positive. The unbelievers, however, were not crushed. They declared that du Bousquier, married or not, had made an excellent sale, for the house had only cost him twenty-seven thousand francs. The believers were depressed by this practical observation of the incredulous. Choisnel, Mademoiselle Cormon's notary, asserted the latter, had heard nothing about the marriage contract; but the believers, still firm in their faith, carried off, on the twentieth day, a signal victory: Monsieur Lepressoir, the notary of the liberals, went to Mademoiselle Cormon's house, and the contract was signed.

This was the first of the numerous sacrifices which Mademoiselle Cormon was destined to make to her husband. Du Bousquier bore the deepest hatred to Choisnel; to him he owed the refusal of the hand of Mademoiselle Armande, - a refusal which, as he believed, had influenced that of Mademoiselle Cormon. This circumstance alone made the marriage drag along. Mademoiselle received several anonymous letters. She learned, to her great astonishment, that Suzanne was as truly a virgin as herself so far as du Bousquier was concerned, for that seducer with the false toupet could never be the hero of any such adventure. Mademoiselle Cormon disdained anonymous letters; but she wrote to Suzanne herself, on the ground of enlightening the Maternity Society. Suzanne, who had no doubt heard of du Bousquier's proposed marriage, acknowledged her trick, sent a thousand francs to the society, and did all the harm she could to the old purveyor. Mademoiselle Cormon convoked the Maternity Society, which held a special meeting at which it was voted that the association would not in future assist any misfortunes about to happen, but solely those that had happened.

In spite of all these various events which kept the town in the choicest gossip, the banns were published in the churches and at the mayor's office. Athanase prepared the deeds. As a matter of propriety and public decency, the bride retired to Prebaudet, where du Bousquier, bearing sumptuous and horrible bouquets, betook himself every morning, returning home for dinner.

At last, on a dull and rainy morning in June, the marriage of Mademoiselle Cormon and the Sieur du Bousquier took place at noon in the parish church of Alencon, in sight of the whole town. The bridal pair went from their own house to the mayor's office, and from the mayor's office to the church in an open caleche, a magnificent vehicle for Alencon, which du Bousquier had sent for secretly to Paris. The loss of the old carriole was a species of calamity in the eyes of the community. The harness-maker of the Porte de Seez bemoaned it, for he lost the fifty francs a year which it cost in repairs. Alencon saw with alarm the possibility of luxury being thus introduced into the town. Every one feared a rise in the price of rents and provisions, and a coming invasion of Parisian furniture. Some persons were sufficiently pricked by curiosity to give ten sous to Jacquelin to allow them a close inspection of the vehicle which threatened to upset the whole economy of the region. A pair of horses, bought in Normandie, were also most alarming.

"If we bought our own horses," said the Ronceret circle, "we couldn't sell them to those who come to buy."

Stupid as it was, this reasoning seemed sound; for surely such a course would prevent the region from grasping the money of foreigners. In the eyes of the provinces wealth consisted less in the rapid turning over of money than in sterile accumulation. It may be mentioned here that Penelope succumbed to a pleurisy which she acquired about six weeks before the marriage; nothing could save her.

Madame Granson, Mariette, Madame du Coudrai, Madame du Ronceret, and through them the whole town, remarked that Madame du Bousquier entered the church *with her left foot*, - an omen all the more dreadful because the term Left was beginning to acquire a political meaning. The priest whose duty it was to read the opening formula opened his book by chance at the De Profundis. Thus the marriage was accompanied by circumstances so fateful, so alarming, so annihilating that no one dared to augur well of it. Matters, in fact, went from bad to worse. There was no wedding party; the married pair departed immediately for Prebaudet. Parisian customs, said the community, were about to triumph over time-honored provincial ways.

The marriage of Jacquelin and Josette now took place: it was gay; and they were the only two persons in Alencon who refuted the sinister prophecies relating to the marriage of their mistress.

Du Bousquier determined to use the proceeds of the sale of his late residence in restoring and modernizing the hotel Cormon. He decided to remain through two seasons at Prebaudet, and took the Abbe de Sponde with them. This news spread terror through the town, where every individual felt that du Bousquier was about to drag the community into the fatal path of "comfort." This fear increased when the inhabitants of Alencon saw the bridegroom driving in from Prebaudet one morning to inspect his works, in a fine tilbury drawn by a new horse, having Rene at his side in livery. The first act of his administration had been to place his wife's savings on the Grand-Livre, which was then quoted at 67 fr. 50 cent. In the space of one year, during which he played constantly for a rise, he made himself a personal fortune almost as considerable as that of his wife.

But all these foreboding prophecies, these perturbing innovations, were superseded and surpassed by an event connected with this marriage which gave a still more fatal aspect to it.

On the very evening of the ceremony, Athanase and his mother were sitting, after their dinner, over a little fire of fagots, which the servant lighted usually at dessert.

"Well, we will go this evening to the du Roncerets', inasmuch as we have lost Mademoiselle Cormon," said Madame Granson. "Heavens! how shall I ever accustom myself to call her Madame du Bousquier! that name burns my lips."

Athanase looked at his mother with a constrained and melancholy air; he could not smile; but he seemed to wish to welcome that naive sentiment which soothed his wound, though it could not cure his anguish.

"Mamma," he said, in the voice of his childhood, so tender was it, and using the name he had abandoned for several years, - "my dear mamma, do not let us go out just yet; it is so pleasant here before the fire."

The mother heard, without comprehending, that supreme prayer of a mortal sorrow.

"Yes, let us stay, my child," she said. "I like much better to talk with you and listen to your projects than to play at boston and lose my money."

"You are so handsome to-night I love to look at you. Besides, I am in a current of ideas which harmonize with this poor little salon where we have suffered so much."

"And where we shall still suffer, my poor Athanase, until your works succeed. For myself, I am trained to poverty; but you, my treasure! to see your youth go by without a joy! nothing but toil for my poor boy in life! That thought is like an illness to a mother; it tortures me at night; it wakes me in the morning. O God! what have I done? for what crime dost thou punish me thus?"

She left her sofa, took a little chair, and sat close to Athanase, so as to lay her head on the bosom of her child. There is always the grace of love in true motherhood. Athanase kissed her on the eyes, on her gray hair, on her forehead, with the sacred desire of laying his soul wherever he applied his lips.

"I shall never succeed," he said, trying to deceive his mother as to the fatal resolution he was revolving in his mind.

"Pooh! don't get discouraged. As you often say, thought can do all things. With ten bottles of ink, ten reams of paper, and his powerful will, Luther upset all Europe. Well, you'll make yourself famous; you will do good things by the same means which he used to do evil things. Haven't you said so yourself? For my part, I listen to you; I understand you a great deal more than you think I do, - for I still bear you in my bosom, and your every thought still stirs me as your slightest motion did in other days."

"I shall never succeed here, mamma; and I don't want you to witness the sight of my struggles, my misery, my anguish. Oh, mother, let me leave Alencon! I want to suffer away from you."

"And I wish to be at your side," replied his mother, proudly. "Suffer without your mother! - that poor mother who would be your servant if necessary; who will efface herself rather than injure you; your mother, who will never shame you. No, no, Athanase; we must not part."

Athanase clung to his mother with the ardor of a dying man who clings to life.

"But I wish it, nevertheless. If not, you will lose me; this double grief, yours and mine, is killing me. You would rather I lived than died?"

Madame Granson looked at her son with a haggard eye.

"So this is what you have been brooding?" she said. "They told me right. Do you really mean to go?"

"Yes."

"You will not go without telling me; without warning me? You must have an outfit and money. I have some louis sewn into my petticoat; I shall give them to you."

Athanase wept.

"That's all I wanted to tell you," he said. "Now I'll take you to the du Roncerets'. Come."

The mother and the son went out. Athanase left his mother at the door of the house where she intended to pass the evening. He looked long at the light which came through the shutters; he clung closely to the wall, and a frenzied joy came over him when he presently heard his mother say, "He has great independence of heart."

"Poor mother! I have deceived her," he cried, as he made his way to the Sarthe.

He reached the noble poplar beneath which he had meditated so much for the last forty days, and where he had placed two heavy stones on which he now sat down. He contemplated that beautiful nature lighted by the moon; he reviewed once more the glorious future he had longed for; he passed through towns that were stirred by his name; he heard the applauding crowds; he breathed the incense of his fame; he adored that life long dreamed of; radiant, he sprang to radiant triumphs; he raised his stature; he evoked his illusions to bid them farewell in a last Olympic feast. The magic had been potent for a moment; but now it vanished forever. In that awful hour he clung to the beautiful tree to which, as to a friend, he had attached himself; then he put the two stones into the pockets of his overcoat, which he buttoned across his breast. He had come intentionally without a hat. He now went to the deep pool he had long selected, and glided into it resolutely, trying to make as little noise as possible, and, in fact, making scarcely any.

When, at half-past nine o'clock, Madame Granson returned home, her servant said nothing of Athanase, but gave her a letter. She opened it and read these few words, -

"My good mother, I have departed; don't be angry with me."

"A pretty trick he has played me!" she thought. "And his linen! and the money! Well, he will write to me, and then I'll follow him. These poor children think they are so much cleverer than their fathers and mothers."

And she went to bed in peace.

During the preceding morning the Sarthe had risen to a height foreseen by the fisherman. These sudden rises of muddy water brought eels from their various runlets. It so happened that a fisherman had spread his net at the very place where poor Athanase had flung himself, believing that no one would ever find him. About six o'clock in the morning the man drew in his net, and with it the young body. The few friends of the poor mother took every precaution in preparing her to receive the dreadful remains. The news of this suicide made, as may well be supposed, a great excitement in Alencon. The poor young man of genius had no protector the night before, but on the morrow of his death a thousand voices cried aloud, "I would have helped him." It is so easy and convenient to be charitable gratis!

The suicide was explained by the Chevalier de Valois. He revealed, in a spirit of revenge, the artless, sincere, and genuine love of Athanase for Mademoiselle Cormon. Madame Granson, enlightened by the chevalier, remembered a thousand little circumstances which confirmed the chevalier's statement. The story then became touching, and many women wept over it. Madame Granson's grief was silent, concentrated, and little understood. There are two forms of mourning for mothers. Often the world can enter fully into the nature of their loss: their son, admired, appreciated, young, perhaps handsome, with a noble path before him, leading to fortune, possibly to fame, excites universal regret; society joins in the grief, and alleviates while it magnifies it. But there is another sorrow of mothers who alone know what their child was really; who alone have received his smiles and observed the treasures of a life too soon cut short. That sorrow hides its woe, the blackness of which surpasses all other mourning; it cannot be described; happily there are but few women whose heart-strings are thus severed.

Before Madame du Bousquier returned to town,

Madame du Ronceret, one of her good friends, had driven out to Prebaudet to fling this corpse upon the roses of her joy, to show her the love she had ignored, and sweetly shed a thousand drops of wormwood into the honey of her bridal month. As Madame du Bousquier drove back to Alencon, she chanced to meet Madame Granson at the corner of the rue Val-Noble. The glance of the mother, dying of her grief, struck to the heart of the poor woman. A thousand maledictions, a thousand flaming reproaches, were in that look: Madame du Bousquier was horror-struck; that glance predicted and called down evil upon her head.

The evening after the catastrophe, Madame Granson, one of the persons most opposed to the rector of the town, and who had hitherto supported the minister of Saint-Leonard, began to tremble as she thought of the inflexible Catholic doctrines professed by her own party. After placing her son's body in its shroud with her own hands, thinking of the mother of the Saviour, she went, with a soul convulsed by anguish, to the house of the hated rector. There she found the modest priest in an outer room, engaged in putting away the flax and yarns with which he supplied poor women, in order that they might never be wholly out of work, - a form of charity which saved many who were incapable of begging from actual penury. The rector left his yarns and hastened to take Madame Granson into his dining-room, where the wretched mother noticed, as she looked at his supper, the frugal method of his own living.

"Monsieur l'abbe," she said, "I have come to implore you -" She burst into tears, unable to continue.

"I know what brings you," replied the saintly man. "I

must trust to you, madame, and to your relation, Madame du Bousquier, to pacify Monseigneur the Bishop at Seez. Yes, I will pray for your unhappy child; yes, I will say the masses. But we must avoid all scandal, and give no opportunity for evil-judging persons to assemble in the church. I alone, without other clergy, at night -"

"Yes, yes, as you think best; if only he may lie in consecrated ground," said the poor mother, taking the priest's hand and kissing it.

Toward midnight a coffin was clandestinely borne to the parish church by four young men, comrades whom Athanase had liked the best. A few friends of Madame Granson, women dressed in black, and veiled, were present; and half a dozen other young men who had been somewhat intimate with this lost genius. Four torches flickered on the coffin, which was covered with crape. The rector, assisted by one discreet choir-boy, said the mortuary mass. Then the body of the suicide was noiselessly carried to a corner of the cemetery, where a black wooden cross, without inscription, was all that indicated its place hereafter to the mother. Athanase lived and died in shadow. No voice was raised to blame the rector; the bishop kept silence. The piety of the mother redeemed the impiety of the son's last act.

Some months later, the poor woman, half beside herself with grief, and moved by one of those inexplicable thirsts which misery feels to steep its lips in the bitter chalice, determined to see the spot where her son was drowned. Her instinct may have told her that thoughts of his could be recovered beneath that poplar; perhaps, too, she desired to see what his eyes had seen for the last time. Some mothers would die of the sight; others give themselves up to it in saintly adoration. Patient anatomists of human nature cannot too often enunciate the truths before which all educations, laws, and philosophical systems must give way. Let us repeat continually: it is absurd to force sentiments into one formula: appearing as they do, in each individual man, they combine with the elements that form his nature and take his own physiognomy.

Madame Granson, as she stood on that fatal spot, saw a woman approach it, who exclaimed, -

"Was it here?"

That woman wept as the mother wept. It was Suzanne. Arriving that morning at the hotel du More, she had been told of the catastrophe. If poor Athanase had been living, she meant to do as many noble souls, who are moneyless, dream of doing, and as the rich never think of doing, - she meant to have sent him several thousand francs, writing up the envelope the words: "Money due to your father from a comrade who makes restitution to you." This tender scheme had been arranged by Suzanne during her journey.

The courtesan caught sight of Madame Granson and moved rapidly away, whispering as she passed her, "I loved him!"

Suzanne, faithful to her nature, did not leave Alencon on this occasion without changing the orange-blossoms of the bride to rue. She was the first to declare that Madame du Bousquier would never be anything but Mademoiselle Cormon. With one stab of her tongue she revenged poor Athanase and her dear chevalier.

Alencon now witnessed a suicide that was slower and quite differently pitiful from that of poor Athanase, who was quickly forgotten by society, which always makes haste to forget its dead. The poor Chevalier de Valois died in life; his suicide was a daily occurrence for fourteen years. Three months after the du Bousquier marriage society remarked, not without astonishment, that the linen of the chevalier was frayed and rusty, that his hair was irregularly combed and brushed. With a frowsy head the Chevalier de Valois could no longer be said to exist! A few of his ivory teeth deserted, though the keenest observers of human life were unable to discover to what body they had hitherto belonged, whether to a foreign legion or whether they were indigenous, vegetable or animal; whether age had pulled them from the chevalier's mouth, or whether they were left forgotten in the drawer of his dressing-table. The cravat was crooked, indifferent to elegance. The negroes' heads grew pale with dust and grease. The wrinkles of the face were blackened and puckered; the skin became parchment. The nails, neglected, were often seen, alas! with a black velvet edging. The waistcoat was tracked and stained with droppings which spread upon its surface like autumn leaves. The cotton in the ears was seldom changed. Sadness reigned upon that brow, and slipped its yellowing tints into the depths of each furrow. In short, the ruins, hitherto so cleverly hidden, now showed through the cracks and crevices of that fine edifice, and proved the power of the soul over the body; for the fair and dainty man, the cavalier, the young blood, died when hope deserted him. Until then the nose of the chevalier was ever delicate and nice; never had a damp black blotch, nor an amber drop fall from it; but now that nose, smeared with tobacco around the nostrils, degraded by the driblets which took advantage of the natural gutter placed between itself and the upper lip, - that nose, which no longer cared to seem agreeable, revealed the infinite pains which the chevalier had formerly taken with his person, and made observers comprehend, by the extent of its degradation, the greatness and persistence of the man's designs upon Mademoiselle Cormon.

Alas, too, the anecdotes went the way of the teeth; the clever sayings grew rare. The appetite, however, remained; the old nobleman saved nothing but his stomach from the wreck of his hopes; though he languidly prepared his pinches of snuff, he ate alarming dinners. Perhaps you will more fully understand the disaster that this marriage was to the mind and heart of the chevalier when you learn that his intercourse with the Princess Goritza became less frequent.

One day he appeared in Mademoiselle Armande's salon with the calf of his leg on the shin-bone. This bankruptcy of the graces was, I do assure you, terrible, and struck all Alencon with horror. The late young man had become an old one; this human being, who, by the breaking-down of his spirit, had passed at once from fifty to ninety years of age, frightened society. Besides, his secret was betrayed; he had waited and watched for Mademoiselle Cormon; he had, like a patient hunter, adjusted his aim for ten whole years, and finally had missed the game! In short, the impotent Republic had won the day from Valiant Chivalry, and that, too, under the Restoration! Form triumphed; mind was vanquished by matter, diplomacy by insurrection. And, O final blow! a mortified grisette revealed the secret of the chevalier's mornings, and he now passed for a libertine. The liberals cast at his door all the foundlings hitherto attributed to du Bousquier. But the faubourg Saint-Germain of Alencon accepted them proudly: it even said, "That poor chevalier, what else could he do?" The faubourg pitied him, gathered him closer to their circle, and brought back a few rare smiles to his face; but frightful enmity was piled upon the head of du Bousquier. Eleven persons deserted the Cormon salon, and passed to that of the d'Esgrignons.

The old maid's marriage had a signal effect in defining the two parties in Alencon. The salon d'Esgrignon represented the upper aristocracy (the returning Troisvilles attached themselves to it); the Cormon salon represented, under the clever influence of du Bousquier, that fatal class of opinions which, without being truly liberal or resolutely royalist, gave birth to the 221 on that famous day when the struggle openly began between the most august, grandest, and only true power, *royalty*, and the most false, most changeful, most oppressive of all powers, - the power called *parliamentary*, which elective assemblies exercise. The salon du Ronceret, secretly allied to the Cormon salon, was boldly liberal.

The Abbe de Sponde, after his return from Prebaudet, bore many and continual sufferings, which he kept within his breast, saying no word of them to his niece. But to Mademoiselle Armande he opened his heart, admitting that, folly for folly, he would much have preferred the Chevalier de Valois to Monsieur du Bousquier. Never would the dear chevalier have had the bad taste to contradict and oppose a poor old man who had but a few days more to live; du Bousquier had destroyed everything in the good old home. The abbe said, with scanty tears moistening his aged eyes, -

"Mademoiselle, I haven't even the little grove where I

have walked for fifty years. My beloved lindens are all cut down! At the moment of my death the Republic appears to me more than ever under the form of a horrible destruction of the Home."

"You must pardon your niece," said the Chevalier de Valois. "Republican ideas are the first error of youth which seeks for liberty; later it finds it the worst of despotisms, - that of an impotent canaille. Your poor niece is punished where she sinned."

"What will become of me in a house where naked women are painted on the walls?" said the poor abbe. "Where shall I find other lindens beneath which to read my breviary?"

Like Kant, who was unable to collect his thoughts after the fir-tree at which he was accustomed to gaze while meditating was cut down, so the poor abbe could never attain the ardor of his former prayers while walking up and down the shadeless paths. Du Bousquier had planted an English garden.

"It was best," said Madame du Bousquier, without thinking so; but the Abbe Couterier had authorized her to commit many wrongs to please her husband.

These restorations destroyed all the venerable dignity, cordiality, and patriarchal air of the old house. Like the Chevalier de Valois, whose personal neglect might be called an abdication, the bourgeois dignity of the Cormon salon no longer existed when it was turned to white and gold, with mahogany ottomans covered in blue satin. The dining-room, adorned in modern taste, was colder in tone than it used to be, and the dinners were eaten with less appetite than formerly. Monsieur du Coudrai declared that he felt his puns stick in his throat as he glanced at the figures painted on the walls, which looked him out of countenance. Externally, the house was still provincial; but internally everything revealed the purveyor of the Directory and the bad taste of the money-changer, - for instance, columns in stucco, glass doors, Greek mouldings, meaningless outlines, all styles conglomerated, magnificence out of place and out of season.

The town of Alencon gabbled for two weeks over this luxury, which seemed unparalleled; but a few months later the community was proud of it, and several rich manufacturers restored their houses and set up fine salons. Modern furniture came into the town, and astral lamps were seen!

The Abbe de Sponde was among the first to perceive the secret unhappiness this marriage now brought to the private life of his beloved niece. The character of noble simplicity which had hitherto ruled their lives was lost during the first winter, when du Bousquier gave two balls every month. Oh, to hear violins and profane music at these worldly entertainments in the sacred old house! The abbe prayed on his knees while the revels lasted. Next the political system of the sober salon was slowly perverted. The abbe fathomed du Bousquier; he shuddered at his imperious tone; he saw the tears in his niece's eyes when she felt herself losing all control over her own property; for her husband now left nothing in her hands but the management of the linen, the table, and things of a kind which are the lot of women. Rose had no longer any orders to give. Monsieur's will was alone regarded by Jacquelin, now become coachman, by Rene, the groom, and by the chef, who came from Paris, Mariette being reduced to kitchen maid. Madame du Bousquier had no one to rule but Josette. Who knows what it costs to relinquish the delights of power? If the triumph of the will is one of the intoxicating pleasures in the lives of great men, it is the ALL of life to narrow minds. One must needs have been a minister dismissed from power to comprehend the bitter pain which came upon Madame du Bousquier when she found herself reduced to this absolute servitude. She often got into the carriage against her will; she saw herself surrounded by servants who were distasteful to her; she no longer had the handling of her dear money, - she who had known herself free to spend money, and did not spend it.

All imposed limits make the human being desire to go beyond them. The keenest sufferings come from the thwarting of self-will. The beginning of this state of things was, however, rose-colored. Every concession made to marital authority was an effect of the love which the poor woman felt for her husband. Du Bousquier behaved, in the first instance, admirably to his wife: he was wise; he was excellent; he gave her the best of reasons for each new encroachment. So for the first two years of her marriage Madame du Bousquier appeared to be satisfied. She had that deliberate, demure little air which distinguishes young women who have married for love. The rush of blood to her head no longer tormented her. This appearance of satisfaction routed the scoffers, contradicted certain rumors about du Bousquier, and puzzled all observers of the human heart. Rose-Marie-Victoire was so afraid that if she displeased her husband or opposed him, she would lose his affection and be deprived of his company, that she would willingly have sacrificed all to him, even her uncle. Her silly little forms of pleasure deceived even the poor abbe for a time, who endured his own trials all the better for thinking that his niece was happy, after all.

Alencon at first thought the same. But there was one man more difficult to deceive than the whole town put together. The Chevalier de Valois, who had taken refuge on the Sacred Mount of the upper aristocracy, now passed his life at the d'Esgrignons. He listened to the gossip and the gabble, and he thought day and night upon his vengeance. He meant to strike du Bousquier to the heart.

The poor abbe fully understood the baseness of this first and last love of his niece; he shuddered as, little by little, he perceived the hypocritical nature of his nephew and his treacherous manoeuvres. Though du Bousquier restrained himself, as he thought of the abbe's property, and wished not to cause him vexation, it was his hand that dealt the blow that sent the old priest to his grave. If you will interpret the word *intolerance* as *firmness of principle*, if you do not wish to condemn in the catholic soul of the Abbe de Sponde the stoicism which Walter Scott has made you admire in the puritan soul of Jeanie Deans' father; if you are willing to recognize in the Roman Church the Potius mori quam foedari that you admire in republican tenets, - you will understand the sorrow of the Abbe de Sponde when he saw in his niece's salon the apostate priest, the renegade, the pervert, the heretic, that enemy of the Church, the guilty taker of the Constitutional oath. Du Bousquier, whose secret ambition was to lay down the law to the town, wished, as a first proof of his power, to reconcile the minister of Saint-Leonard with the rector of the parish, and he succeeded. His wife thought he had accomplished a work of peace where the immovable abbe saw only treachery. The bishop came to visit du Bousquier, and seemed glad of the cessation of hostilities. The virtues of the Abbe Francois had conquered prejudice, except that of the aged Roman Catholic, who exclaimed with Cornelle, "Alas! what virtues do you make me hate!"

The abbe died when orthodoxy thus expired in the diocese.

In 1819, the property of the Abbe de Sponde increased Madame du Bousquier's income from real estate to twenty-five thousand francs without counting Prebaudet or the house in the Val-Noble. About this time du Bousquier returned to his wife the capital of her savings which she had yielded to him; and he made her use it in purchasing lands contiguous to Prebaudet, which made that domain one of the most considerable in the department, for the estates of the Abbe de Sponde also adjoined it. Du Bousquier thus passed for one of the richest men of the department. This able man, the constant candidate of the liberals, missing by seven or eight votes only in all the electoral battles fought under the Restoration, and who ostensibly repudiated the liberals by trying to be elected as a ministerial royalist (without ever being able to conquer the aversion of the administration), - this rancorous republican, mad with ambition, resolved to rival the royalism and aristocracy of Alencon at the moment when they once more had the upper hand. He strengthened himself with the Church by the deceitful appearance of a well-feigned piety: he accompanied his wife to mass; he gave money for the convents of the town; he assisted the congregation of the Sacre-Coeur; he took sides with the clergy on all occasions when the clergy came into collision with the town, the department, or the State. Secretly supported by the liberals, protected by the Church, calling himself a constitutional royalist, he kept beside the aristocracy of the department in the one hope of ruining it, - and he did ruin it. Ever on the watch for the faults and blunders of the nobility and the government, he laid plans for his vengeance against the "chateau-people," and especially against the d'Esgrignons, in whose bosom he was one day to thrust a poisoned dagger.

Among other benefits to the town he gave money liberally to revive the manufacture of point d'Alencon; he renewed the trade in linens, and the town had a factory. Inscribing himself thus upon the interests and heart of the masses, by doing what the royalists did not do, du Bousquier did not really risk a farthing. Backed by his fortune, he could afford to wait results which enterprising persons who involve themselves are forced to abandon to luckier successors.

Du Bousquier now posed as a banker. This miniature Lafitte was a partner in all new enterprises, taking good security. He served himself while apparently serving the interests of the community. He was the prime mover of insurance companies, the protector of new enterprises for public conveyance; he suggested petitions for asking the administration for the necessary roads and bridges. Thus warned, the government considered this action an encroachment of its own authority. A struggle was begun injudiciously, for the good of the community compelled the authorities to yield in the end. Du Bousquier embittered the provincial nobility against the court nobility and the peerage; and finally he brought about the shocking adhesion of a strong party of constitutional royalists to the warfare sustained by the "Journal des Debats," and M. de Chateaubriand against the throne, - an ungrateful opposition based on ignoble interests, which was one cause of the triumph of the bourgeoisie and journalism in 1830.

Thus du Bousquier, in common with the class he represented, had the satisfaction of beholding the funeral of royalty. The old republican, smothered with masses, who for fifteen years had played that comedy to satisfy his vendetta, himself threw down with his own hand the white flag of the mayoralty to the applause of the multitude. No man in France cast upon the new throne raised in August, 1830, a glance of more intoxicated, joyous vengeance. The accession of the Younger Branch was the triumph of the Revolution. To him the victory of the tricolor meant the resurrection of Montagne, which this time should surely bring the nobility down to the dust by means more certain than that of the guillotine, because less violent. The peerage without heredity; the National Guard, which puts on the same camp-bed the corner grocer and the marquis; the abolition of the entails demanded by a bourgeois lawyer; the Catholic Church deprived of its supremacy; and all the other legislative inventions of August, 1830, - were to du Bousquier the wisest possible application of the principles of 1793.

Since 1830 this man has been a receiver-general. He relied for his advancement on his relations with the Duc d'Orleans, father of Louis Philippe, and with Monsieur de Folmon, formerly steward to the Duchess-dowager of Orleans. He receives about eighty thousand francs a year. In the eyes of the people about him Monsieur du Bousquier is a man of means, - a respectable man, steady in his principles, upright, and obliging. Alencon owes to him its connection with the industrial movement by which Brittany may possibly some day be joined to what is popularly called modern civilization. Alencon, which up to 1816 could boast of only two private carriages, saw, without amazement, in the course of ten years, coupes, landaus, tilburies, and cabriolets rolling through her streets. The burghers and the land-owners, alarmed at first lest the price of everything should increase, recognized later that this increase in the style of living had a contrary effect upon their revenues. The prophetic remark of du Ronceret, "Du Bousquier is a very strong man," was adopted by the whole country-side.

But, unhappily for the wife, that saying has a double meaning. The husband does not in any way resemble the public politician. This great citizen, so liberal to the world about him, so kindly inspired with love for his native place, is a despot in his own house, and utterly devoid of conjugal affection. This man, so profoundly astute, hypocritical, and sly; this Cromwell of the Val-Noble, - behaves in his home as he behaves to the aristocracy, whom he caresses in hopes to throttle them. Like his friend Bernadotte, he wears a velvet glove upon his iron hand. His wife has given him no children. Suzanne's remark and the chevalier's insinuations were therefore justified. But the liberal bourgeoisie, the constitutional-royalist-bourgeoisie, the country-squires, the magistracy, and the "church party" laid the blame on Madame du Bousquier. "She was too old," they said; "Monsieur du Bousquier had married her too late. Besides, it was very lucky for the poor woman; it was dangerous at her age to bear children!" When Madame du Bousquier confided, weeping, her periodic despair to Mesdames du Coudrai and du Ronceret, those ladies would reply, -

"But you are crazy, my dear; you don't know what you

are wishing for; a child would be your death."

Many men, whose hopes were fastened on du Bousquier's triumph, sang his praises to their wives, who in turn repeated them to the poor wife in some such speech as this: -

"You are very lucky, dear, to have married such an able man; you'll escape the misery of women whose husbands are men without energy, incapable of managing their property, or bringing up their children."

"Your husband is making you queen of the department, my love. He'll never leave you embarrassed, not he! Why, he leads all Alencon."

"But I wish," said the poor wife, "that he gave less time to the public and -"

"You are hard to please, my dear Madame du Bousquier. I assure you that all the women in town envy you your husband."

Misjudged by society, which began by blaming her, the pious woman found ample opportunity in her home to display her virtues. She lived in tears, but she never ceased to present to others a placid face. To so Christian a soul a certain thought which pecked forever at her heart was a crime: "I loved the Chevalier de Valois," it said; "but I have married du Bousquier." The love of poor Athanase Granson also rose like a phantom of remorse, and pursued her even in her dreams. The death of her uncle, whose griefs at the last burst forth, made her life still more sorrowful; for she now felt the suffering her uncle must have endured in witnessing the change of political and religious opinion in the old house. Sorrow often falls like a thunderbolt, as it did on Madame Granson; but in this old maid it slowly spread like a drop of oil, which never leaves the stuff that slowly imbibes it.

The Chevalier de Valois was the malicious manipulator who brought about the crowning misfortune of Madame du Bousquier's life. His heart was set on undeceiving her pious simplicity; for the chevalier, expert in love, divined du Bousquier, the married man, as he had divined du Bousquier, the bachelor. But the wary republican was difficult of attack. His salon was, of course, closed to the Chevalier de Valois, as to all those who, in the early days of his marriage, had slighted the Cormon mansion. He was, moreover, impervious to ridicule; he possessed a vast fortune; he reigned in Alencon; he cared as little for his wife as Richard III. cared for the dead horse which had helped him win a battle. To please her husband, Madame du Bousquier had broken off relations with the d'Esgrignon household, where she went no longer, except that sometimes when her husband left her during his trips to Paris, she would pay a brief visit to Mademoiselle Armande.

About three years after her marriage, at the time of the Abbe de Sponde's death, Mademoiselle Armande joined Madame du Bousquier as they were leaving Saint-Leonard's, where they had gone to hear a requiem said for him. The generous demoiselle thought that on this occasion she owed her sympathy to the niece in trouble. They walked together, talking of the dear deceased, until they reached the forbidden house, into which Mademoiselle Armande enticed Madame du Bousquier by the charm of her manner and conversation. The poor desolate woman was glad to talk of her uncle with one whom he truly loved. Moreover, she wanted to receive the condolences of the old marquis, whom she had not seen for nearly three years. It was half-past one o'clock, and she found at the hotel d'Esgrignon the Chevalier de Valois, who had come to dinner. As he bowed to her, he took her by the hands.

"Well, dear, virtuous, and beloved lady," he said, in a tone of emotion, "we have lost our sainted friend; we share your grief. Yes, your loss is as keenly felt here as in your own home, - more so," he added, alluding to du Bousquier.

After a few more words of funeral oration, in which all present spoke from the heart, the chevalier took Madame du Bousquier's arm, and, gallantly placing it within his own, pressed it adoringly as he led her to the recess of a window.

"Are you happy?" he said in a fatherly voice.

"Yes," she said, dropping her eyes.

Hearing that "Yes," Madame de Troisville, the daughter of the Princess Scherbellof, and the old Marquise de Casteran came up and joined the chevalier, together with Mademoiselle Armande. They all went to walk in the garden until dinner was served, without any perception on the part of Madame du Bousquier that a little conspiracy was afoot. "We have her! now let us find out the secret of the case," were the words written in the eyes of all present.

"To make your happiness complete," said Mademoiselle Armande, "you ought to have children, - a fine lad like my nephew -"

Tears seemed to start in Madame du Bousquier's eyes.

"I have heard it said that you were the one to blame in the matter, and that you feared the dangers of a pregnancy," said the chevalier.

"I!" she said artlessly. "I would buy a child with a hundred years of purgatory if I could."

On the question thus started a discussion arose, conducted by Madame de Troisville and the old Marquise de Casteran with such delicacy and adroitness that the poor victim revealed, without being aware of it, the secrets of her house. Mademoiselle Armande had taken the chevalier's arm, and walked away so as to leave the three women free to discuss wedlock. Madame du Bousquier was then enlightened on the various deceptions of her marriage; and as she was still the same simpleton she had always been, she amused her advisers by delightful naivetes.

Although at first the deceptive marriage of Mademoiselle Cormon made a laugh throughout the town, which was soon initiated into the story of the case, before long Madame du Bousquier won the esteem and sympathy of all the women. The fact that Mademoiselle Cormon had flung herself headlong into marriage without succeeding in being married, made everybody laugh at her; but when they learned the exceptional position in which the sternness of her religious principles placed her, all the world admired her. "That poor Madame du Bousquier" took the place of "That good Mademoiselle Cormon."

Thus the chevalier contrived to render du Bousquier both ridiculous and odious for a time; but ridicule ends by weakening; when all had said their say about him, the gossip died out. Besides, at fifty-seven years of age the dumb republican seemed to many people to have a right to retire. This affair, however, envenomed the hatred which du Bousquier already bore to the house of Esgrignon to such a degree that it made him pitiless when the day of vengeance came. [See "The Gallery of Antiquities."] Madame du Bousquier received orders never again to set foot into that house. By way of reprisals upon the chevalier for the trick thus played him, du Bousquier, who had just created the journal called the "Courrier de l'Orne," caused the following notice to be inserted in it: -

"Bonds to the amount of one thousand francs a year will be paid to any person who can prove the existence of one Monsieur de Pombreton before, during, or after the Emigration."

Although her marriage was essentially negative, Madame du Bousquier saw some advantages in it: was it not better to interest herself in the most remarkable man in the town than to live alone? Du Bousquier was preferable to a dog, or cat, or those canaries that spinsters love. He showed for his wife a sentiment more real and less selfish than that which is felt by servants, confessors, and hopeful heirs. Later in life she came to consider her husband as the instrument of divine wrath; for she then saw innumerable sins in her former desires for marriage; she regarded herself as justly punished for the sorrow she had brought on Madame Granson, and for the hastened death of her uncle. Obedient to that religion which commands us to kiss the rod with which the punishment is inflicted, she praised her husband, and publicly approved him. But in the confessional, or at night, when praying, she wept often, imploring God's forgiveness for the apostasy of the man who thought the contrary of what he professed, and who desired the destruction of the aristocracy and the Church, - the two religions of the house of Cormon.

With all her feelings bruised and immolated within her, compelled by duty to make her husband happy, attached to him by a certain indefinable affection, born, perhaps, of habit, her life became one perpetual contradiction. She had married a man whose conduct and opinions she hated, but whom she was bound to care for with dutiful tenderness. Often she walked with the angels when du Bousquier ate her preserves or thought the dinner good. She watched to see that his slightest wish was satisfied. If he tore off the cover of his newspaper and left it on a table, instead of throwing it away, she would say: -

"Rene, leave that where it is; monsieur did not place it there without intention."

If du Bousquier had a journey to take, she was anxious about his trunk, his linen; she took the most minute precautions for his material benefit. If he went to Prebaudet, she consulted the barometer the evening before to know if the weather would be fine. She watched for his will in his eyes, like a dog which hears and sees its master while sleeping. When the stout du Bousquier, touched by this scrupulous love, would take her round the waist and kiss her forehead, saying, "What a good woman you are!" tears of pleasure would come into the eyes of the poor creature. It is probably that du Bousquier felt himself obliged to make certain concessions which obtained for him the respect of Rose-Marie-Victoire; for Catholic virtue does not require a dissimulation as complete as that of Madame du Bousquier. Often the good saint sat mutely by and listened to the hatred of men who concealed themselves under the cloak of constitutional royalists. She shuddered as she foresaw the ruin of the Church. Occasionally she risked a stupid word, an observation which du Bousquier cut short with a glance.

The worries of such an existence ended by stupefying Madame du Bousquier, who found it easier and also more dignified to concentrate her intelligence on her own thoughts and resign herself to lead a life that was purely animal. She then adopted the submission of a slave, and regarded it as a meritorious deed to accept the degradation in which her husband placed her. The fulfilment of his will never once caused her to murmur. The timid sheep went henceforth in the way the shepherd led her; she gave herself up to the severest religious practices, and thought no more of Satan and his works and vanities. Thus she presented to the eyes of the world a union of all Christian virtues; and du Bousquier was certainly one of the luckiest men in the kingdom of France and of Navarre.

"She will be a simpleton to her last breath," said the former collector, who, however, dined with her twice a week.

This history would be strangely incomplete if no mention were made of the coincidence of the Chevalier de Valois's death occurring at the same time as that of Suzanne's mother. The chevalier died with the monarchy, in August, 1830. He had joined the cortege of Charles X. at Nonancourt, and piously escorted it to

Cherbourg with the Troisvilles, Casterans, d'Esgrig-nons, Verneuils, etc. The old gentleman had taken with him fifty thousand francs, - the sum to which his savings then amounted. He offered them to one of the faithful friends of the king for transmission to his master, speaking of his approaching death, and declaring that the money came originally from the goodness of the king, and, moreover, that the property of the last of the Valois belonged of right to the crown. It is not known whether the fervor of his zeal conquered the reluctance of the Bourbon, who abandoned his fine kingdom of France without carrying away with him a farthing, and who ought to have been touched by the devotion of the chevalier. It is certain, however, that Cesarine, the residuary legate of the old man, received from his estate only six hundred francs a year. The chevalier returned to Alencon, cruelly weakened by grief and by fatigue; he died on the very day when Charles X. arrived on a foreign shore.

Madame du Val-Noble and her protector, who was just then afraid of the vengeance of the liberal party, were glad of a pretext to remain incognito in the village where Suzanne's mother died. At the sale of the chevalier's effects, which took place at that time, Suzanne, anxious to obtain a souvenir of her first and last friend, pushed up the price of the famous snuff-box, which was finally knocked down to her for a thousand francs. The portrait of the Princess Goritza was alone worth that sum. Two years later, a young dandy, who was making a collection of the fine snuff-boxes of the last century, obtained from Madame du Val-Noble the chevalier's treasure. The charming confidant of many a love and the pleasure of an old age is now on exhibition in a species of private museum. If the dead could know what happens after them, the chevalier's head would surely blush upon its left cheek.

If this history has no other effect than to inspire the possessors of precious relics with holy fear, and induce them to make codicils to secure these touching souvenirs of joys that are no more by bequeathing them to loving hands, it will have done an immense service to the chivalrous and romantic portion of the community; but it does, in truth, contain a far higher moral. Does it not show the necessity for a new species of education? Does it not invoke, from the enlightened solicitude of the ministers of Public Instruction, the creation of chairs of anthropology, - a science in which Germany outstrips us? Modern myths are even less understood than ancient ones, harried as we are with myths. Myths are pressing us from every point; they serve all theories, they explain all questions. They are, according to human ideas, the torches of history; they would save empires from revolution if only the professors of history would force the explanations they give into the mind of the provincial masses. If Mademoiselle Cormon had been a reader or a student, and if there had existed in the department of the Orne a professor of anthropology, or even had she read Ariosto, the frightful disasters of her conjugal life would never have occurred. She would probably have known why the Italian poet makes Angelica prefer Medoro, who was a blond Chevalier de Valois, to Orlando, whose mare was dead, and who knew no better than to fly into a passion. Is not Medoro the mythic form for all courtiers of feminine royalty, and Orlando the myth of disorderly, furious, and impotent revolutions, which destroy but cannot produce? We publish, but without assuming any responsibility for it, this opinion of a pupil of Monsieur Ballanche.

No information has reached us as to the fate of the negroes' heads in diamonds. You may see Madame du Val-Noble every evening at the Opera. Thanks to the education given her by the Chevalier de Valois, she has almost the air of a well-bred woman.

Madame du Bousquier still lives; is not that as much as to say she still suffers? After reaching the age of sixty - the period at which women allow themselves to make confessions - she said confidentially to Madame du Coudrai, that she had never been able to endure the idea of dying an old maid.

Choose from Thousands of 1stWorldLibrary Classics By

Adolphus WilliamWard
Aesop
Agatha Christie
Alexander Aaronsohn
Alexander Kielland
Alexandre Dumas
Alfred Gatty
Alfred Ollivant
Alice Duer Miller
Alice Turner Curtis
Alice Dunbar
Ambrose Bierce
Amelia E. Barr
Andrew Lang
Andrew McFarland Davis
Anna Sewell
Annie Besant
Annie Hamilton Donnell
Annie Payson Call
Anton Chekhov
Arnold Bennett
Arthur Conan Doyle
Arthur Ransome
Atticus
B. M. Bower
Basil King
Bayard Taylor
Ben Macomber
Booth Tarkington
Bram Stoker
C. Collodi
C. E. Orr
C. M. Ingleby
Carolyn Wells
Catherine Parr Traill
Charles A. Eastman
Charles Dickens
Charles Dudley Warner
Charles Farrar Browne
Charles Ives
Charles Kingsley
Charles Lathrop Pack
Charles Whibley
Charles Willing Beale
Charlotte M. Braeme
Charlotte M.Yonge
Clair W. Hayes
Clarence Day Jr.
Clarence E. Mulford

Clemence Housman
Confucius
Cornelis DeWitt Wilcox
Cyril Burleigh
D. H. Lawrence
Daniel Defoe
David Garnett
Don Carlos Janes
Donald Keyhole
Dorothy Kilner
Dougan Clark
E. Nesbit
E.P.Roe
E. Phillips Oppenheim
Edgar Allan Poe
Edgar Rice Burroughs
Edith Wharton
Edward J. O'Biren
John Cournos
Edwin L. Arnold
Eleanor Atkins
Elizabeth Cleghorn
Gaskell
Elizabeth Von Arnim
Ellem Key
Emily Dickinson
Erasmus W. Jones
Ernie Howard Pie
Ethel Turner
Ethel Watts Mumford
Eugenie Foa
Eugene Wood
Evelyn Everett-Green
Everard Cotes
F. J. Cross
Federick Austin Ogg
Ferdinand Ossendowski
Francis Bacon
Francis Darwin
Frances Hodgson Burnett
Frank Gee Patchin
Frank Harris
Frank Jewett Mather
Frank L. Packard
Frederick Trevor Hill
Frederick Winslow Taylor
Friedrich Kerst
Friedrich Nietzsche
Fyodor Dostoyevsky

Gabrielle E. Jackson
Garrett P. Serviss
Gaston Leroux
George Ade
Geroge Bernard Shaw
George Ebers
George Eliot
George MacDonald
George Orwell
George Tucker
George W. Cable
George Wharton James
Gertrude Atherton
Grace E. King
Grant Allen
Guillermo A. Sherwell
Gulielma Zollinger
Gustav Flaubert
H. A. Cody
H. B. Irving
H. G. Wells
H. H. Munro
H. Irving Hancock
H. Rider Haggard
H. W. C. Davis
Hamilton Wright Mabie
Hans Christian Andersen
Harold Avery
Harold McGrath
Harriet Beecher Stowe
Harry Houidini
Helent Hunt Jackson
Helen Nicolay
Hendy David Thoreau
Henrik Ibsen
Henry Adams
Henry Ford
Henry Frost
Henry James
Henry Jones Ford
Henry Seton Merriman
Henry Wadsworth
Longfellow
Henry W Longfellow
Herbert A. Giles
Herbert N. Casson
Herman Hesse
Homer
Honore De Balzac

Horace Walpole
Horatio Alger, Jr.
Howard Pyle
Howard R. Garis
Hugh Lofting
Hugh Walpole
Humphry Ward
Ian Maclaren
Israel Abrahams
J.G.Austin
J. Henri Fabre
J. M. Barrie
J. Macdonald Oxley
J. S. Knowles
J. Storer Clouston
Jack London
Jacob Abbott
James Allen
James Lane Allen
James Andrews
James Baldwin
James DeMille
James Joyce
James Oliver Curwood
James Oppenheim
James Otis
Jane Austen
Jens Peter Jacobsen
Jerome K. Jerome
John Burroughs
John F. Kennedy
John Gay
John Glasworthy
John Habberton
John Joy Bell
John Milton
John Philip Sousa
Jonathan Swift
Joseph Carey
Joseph Conrad
Joseph Jacobs
Julian Hawthrone
Julies Vernes
Justin Huntly McCarthy
Kakuzo Okakura
Kenneth Grahame
Kate Langley Bosher
L. A. Abbot
L. T. Meade
L. Frank Baum
Laura Lee Hope

Laurence Housman
Leo Tolstoy
Leonid Andreyev
Lewis Carroll
Lilian Bell
Lloyd Osbourne
Louis Tracy
Louisa May Alcott
Lucy Fitch Perkins
Lucy Maud Montgomery
Lydia Miller Middleton
Lyndon Orr
M. H. Adams
Margaret E. Sangster
Margaret Vandercook
Maria Edgeworth
Maria Thompson Daviess
Mariano Azuela
Marion Polk Angellotti
Mark Overton
Mark Twain
Mary Austin
Mary Cole
Mary Rowlandson
Mary Wollstonecraft
Shelley
Max Beerbohm
Myra Kelly
Nathaniel Hawthrone
O. F. Walton
Oscar Wilde
Owen Johnson
P.G.Wodehouse
Paul and Mable Thorn
Paul G. Tomlinson
Paul Severing
Peter B. Kyne
Plato
R. Derby Holmes
R. L. Stevenson
Rabindranath Tagore
Rahul Alvares
Ralph Waldo Emmerson
Rene Descartes
Rex E. Beach
Richard Harding Davis
Richard Jefferies
Robert Barr
Robert Frost
Robert Gordon Anderson
Robert L. Drake

Robert Lansing
Robert Michael Ballantyne
Robert W. Chambers
Rosa Nouchette Carey
Ross Kay
Rudyard Kipling
Samuel B. Allison
Samuel Hopkins Adams
Sarah Bernhardt
Selma Lagerlof
Sherwood Anderson
Sigmund Freud
Standish O'Grady
Stanley Weyman
Stella Benson
Stephen Crane
Stewart Edward White
Stijn Streuvels
Swami Abhedananda
Swami Parmananda
T. S. Ackland
The Princess Der Ling
Thomas A. Janvier
Thomas A Kempis
Thomas Anderton
Thomas Bailey Aldrich
Thomas Bulfinch
Thomas De Quincey
Thomas H. Huxley
Thomas Hardy
Thomas More
Thornton W. Burgess
U. S. Grant
Valentine Williams
Victor Appleton
Virginia Woolf
Walter Scott
Washington Irving
Wilbur Lawton
Wilkie Collins
Willa Cather
Willard F. Baker
William Makepeace
Thackeray
William W. Walter
Winston Churchill
Yei Theodora Ozaki
Young E. Allison
Zane Grey